Dear Reader,

We're thrilled that some of Harlequin's most famous families are making an encore appearance! With this special Famous Families fifty-book collection, we are proud to offer you the chance to relive the drama, the glamour, the suspense and the romance of four of Harlequin's most beloved families—the Fortunes, the Bravos, the McCabes and the Cavanaughs.

Our third family, the McCabes, welcomes you to Laramie, Texas. A small ranching town of brick buildings, awnings and shady streets, Laramie is the kind of place where everyone knows each other. The little town is currently abuzz with wedding plans—and no McCabe is safe from the matchmaking! The path to the altar may not be smooth for the McCabes, but their humor-filled journeys will no doubt bring a smile to your face.

And in August, you'll be captivated by our final family, the Cavanaughs. Generations of Cavanaughs have protected the citizens of Aurora, California. But can they protect themselves from falling in love? You won't want to miss any of these stories from *USA TODAY* bestselling author Marie Ferrarella!

Happy reading,

The Editors

CATHY GILLEN THACKER

is married and a mother of three. She and her
husband spent eighteen years in Texas and now
reside in North Carolina. Her mysteries, romantic
comedies and heartwarming family stories have
made numerous appearances on bestseller lists,
but her best reward, she says, is knowing one of her
books made someone's day a little brighter.

A popular Harlequin Books author for many years,
she loves telling passionate stories with happy
endings, and thinks nothing beats a good romance
and a hot cup of tea! You can visit Cathy's website
at www.cathygillenthacker.com for more information
on her upcoming and previously published books,
recipes and a list of her favorite things.

FAMOUS FAMILIES
the McCABES

CATHY GILLEN THACKER

Dr. Cowboy

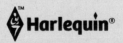

TORONTO NEW YORK LONDON
AMSTERDAM PARIS SYDNEY HAMBURG
STOCKHOLM ATHENS TOKYO MILAN MADRID
PRAGUE WARSAW BUDAPEST AUCKLAND

Recycling programs
for this product may
not exist in your area.

ISBN-13: 978-0-373-36504-3

DR. COWBOY

Copyright © 1999 by Cathy Gillen Thacker

This edition published by arrangement with Harlequin Books S.A.

For questions and comments about the quality of this book
please contact us at Customer_eCare@Harlequin.ca.

www.Harlequin.com

Printed in U.S.A.

FAMOUS FAMILIES

The Fortunes

Cowboy at Midnight by Ann Major
A Baby Changes Everything by Marie Ferrarella
In the Arms of the Law by Peggy Moreland
Lone Star Rancher by Laurie Paige
The Good Doctor by Karen Rose Smith
The Debutante by Elizabeth Bevarly
Keeping Her Safe by Myrna Mackenzie
The Law of Attraction by Kristi Gold
Once a Rebel by Sheri WhiteFeather
Military Man by Marie Ferrarella
Fortune's Legacy by Maureen Child
The Reckoning by Christie Ridgway

The Bravos by Christine Rimmer

The Nine-Month Marriage
Marriage by Necessity
Practically Married
Married by Accident
The Millionaire She Married
The M.D. She Had to Marry
The Marriage Agreement
The Bravo Billionaire
The Marriage Conspiracy
His Executive Sweetheart
Mercury Rising
Scrooge and the Single Girl

Chapter 1

The six-foot-high, bachelor party cake was wheeled out of the backroom of the Laramie, Texas, saloon to the raucous accompaniment of "The Stripper." *Baum, baum, baum* the brass blared with rowdy familiarity as the blood pressure of every man in the room—including Jackson McCabe's—rose in anticipation. *Bah-bah-bah-baum...*

"Oh, Lord, you boys have done it now," sixty-three-year-old Doc McCabe said, rolling his eyes as perspiration broke out on his neck.

"When your mother finds out about this she's gonna tan your hides."

"Not to worry, Dad," Shane—the wildest of the four McCabe boys—drawled. "We didn't hire the stripper. Isabel, over at the bakery, did."

"Even worse!" Doc scowled at his four strapping

sons. "Isabel and her daughter are friends of ours, you know."

Jackson had heard about Isabel Buchanon's daughter, even though they'd never met. Isabel might be the nicest newcomer to grace Laramie in years but Lacey was as pushy as could be. He wanted no part of her. Jackson leaned back against the bar and grinned at his dad over the rim of his beer mug. "Relax and enjoy yourself, Dad. We certainly plan to." He and his three brothers guffawed and elbowed each other as another drum roll sounded, sexy as all get-out.

Doc shook his head in silent remonstration and did his best to quash an amused smile as he kept his eyes on the cake. Slowly the lid opened. *Bah-bah-bah. Dah-dah-dah-dah.* A snazzy white Stetson emerged, followed by the face of an angel framed by a wealth of glossy honey-blond hair.

Jackson took another sip of beer to soothe the sudden dryness of his throat as he cataloged the features of the evening's highly paid entertainment: slender shoulders encased in a fringed cowgirl dress that in no way detracted from her high round breasts and slender waist; curvacious hips that shimmied in time to the music; and legs… Man alive. Jackson sighed wistfully and shook his head. Heaven's above. Legs that would put a Dallas Cowboys cheerleader's to shame.

Dah-bump! Dah-bump! While his pulse raced, and lower still, heat pooled with erotic accuracy, the stripper lifted one leg out of the cake and stepped over onto the bar. Dancing across the top, she stopped at the center, as "The Stripper" music cranked up for another chorus. Tossing her head, she pranced back and forth, doing the meanest bump-and-grind Jackson had ever seen. But instead of stopping in front of Jackson's dad, removing his Stetson and exchanging it for hers, as had been requested by Jackson and his brothers, she leaned down, took off *Jackson's* Stetson, tossed it into the crowd and put her hat on Jackson's head.

Aw, heck, Jackson swore silently to himself, frustrated not to be able to respond the way he'd like to. "You've got the wrong guy," Jackson mouthed to the gyrating stripper over the raucous pounding of the bawdy music.

Not missing a single beat, and looking all the more pleased with herself—and him—she mouthed right back, "I don't think so."

Jackson grasped her shoulders, doing his level best to ignore the delicious, womanly scent of her, and brought her close enough to shout in her ear, "The party's for my dad."

Smiling mysteriously, she drew back and announced loudly enough for everyone to hear. "But this, cowboy, is for you."

Then, with excruciating slowness, she unbuttoned the front of her dress, still gyrating to the sexy music all the while. Jackson's mouth went even dryer. Before he could stop her, she popped it open. To hoots and whistles she let the fringed leather dress fall to her feet. Her curves spilling over the top of a gold lamé bikini, she put her hands on his shoulders and her mouth next to his ear. "Help me down, cowboy," she said.

Figuring, What the hell, it was too late to stop her now, Jackson slid his hands around her waist, and did as she had asked. As soon as her boots touched the floor, he let her go.

She grabbed her dress in one hand and headed for his dad.

"Congratulations on your retirement." She spoke in John McCabe's ear and stood on tiptoe to kiss his creased, suntanned cheek. "And good luck on the renewal of your wedding vows with Lilah, coming up next month."

"Thanks, honey." To Jackson's amazement, his dad hugged the stripper and returned her kiss, just as affectionately, on the cheek.

Did the two of them know each other? Jackson wondered as he set his empty beer mug on the bar. Or was this just good-ol' Texas hospitality at work?

With the music still rolling, the stripper swiveled back to Jackson and turned the full impact of her long-lashed green eyes on him. She clamped a silky hand around his wrist and said in a deep sultry voice that had his engine revving even more, "Now it's your turn, cowboy."

Jackson grinned at the promise in her low, sexy voice, beginning to see that the good-natured prank was on him after all. "For what?" he drawled, both intrigued and amused.

"You'll see." With a broad wink, she headed for the backroom, Jackson in tow. "See you later, fellas," she called flirtatiously over her shoulder.

Hoots and catcalls abounded as Jackson let himself be led into the saloon's backroom. The door shut behind him. The music on the intercom went from "The Stripper" to Garth Brooks's "Friends In Low

Places." An apt selection, Jackson thought as he regarded the beautiful stripper whose soft, feminine hand was still manacled silkily about his wrist.

"Now what?" he asked, wondering where all this was going.

Reluctantly she let go of him, then gestured gracefully toward the old-fashioned, wooden swivel chair behind the desk. "Why don't you sit down and we'll see."

Jackson appreciated a pretty woman as much as the next guy, but when it came to the women he got involved with, physically or otherwise, he had standards. Impossibly high ones, as his friends, family and colleagues were quick to tease. Jackson tore his eyes from her luscious body and did his best to let her down gently.

"The joke's over." He gauged her expression. "Or is it?" he asked carefully, noting she didn't seem about to give up despite his dismissal.

She batted her eyes at him flirtatiously and smoothed a hand provocatively down the front of his shirt causing his heart to pound all the more.

"You aren't afraid of me, are you?"

Jackson felt himself tense even as he disabused her of that notion promptly. "Course not." He regarded her gruffly, doing his best to ignore the provocative floral notes of her perfume. It wasn't likely his father, one of the most respected doctors in central Texas, would hire an actual hooker—even at a stag party. Would he? No, Jackson told himself firmly, this had to be someone from the singing telegram agency they'd asked Isabel to contact, who had merely been paid again by some-

one else to turn the tables on him. From the looks of
things, Jackson noted with mounting frustration, she
wasn't about to leave until she had carried out the joke
to the end. And they were probably about there already,
he thought.

She curved her bow-shaped lips into a sultry smile.
"Then sit."

Figuring the sooner he cooperated, the sooner the
joke would be over—at least his part in it—Jackson
dropped lazily into the chair.

"Ever play cowboys and cowgirls as a kid?" she
asked, still batting her long lashes at him.

Jackson eyed the coiled length of rope she picked
up from the credenza behind the desk. "Not like this,"
he replied.

But he supposed he could play along, at least for a
few more minutes. He didn't want to hurt her feelings.
And it was clear she was trying awfully hard to entice
him.

"Then you're in for a treat."

That was debatable, Jackson thought, his patience
for all the tomfoolery beginning to wear thin as she
playfully took his wrists and forced them behind the
chair. As swiftly as a cowpuncher readying a calf for
branding, she'd looped them together, wrapped the rope
around his midsection and secured the rest of him to
the chair. "You know, if you're planning to rob the
place—or me," he drawled, stretching his long legs
out in front of him lazily, "I think I should warn you,
the sheriff is right out there."

"I don't want to steal anything from you, Jackson."

She slipped on her dress and quickly buttoned up the front.

Jackson lamented the change in scenery. She'd looked damn good just wearing a bikini and boots. He flexed his broad shoulders restlessly against the hard, wooden back of the chair. "Then what do you want?"

Suddenly, her manner became a lot more direct. Disturbingly so. "Your cooperation."

"Cooperation." Jackson repeated her words warily, sensing some kind of scam coming on. "In what?" he demanded roughly.

Lacey plucked her hat off his head and put it back on her head. She hoisted herself up on the edge of the desk and smiled at him bluntly. "The proposal I have to make."

He narrowed his eyes. Now he knew he'd been had. "Who the hell are you?" he demanded hotly.

With the tip of an index finger, she tipped her hat farther back on her head. "Lacey Buchanon, cowboy. Dr. Lacey Buchanon to you."

As her name sank in, Jackson struggled against the coils of rope wound around his middle and let loose a string of colorful swear words. "Oh, no," he said hotly. "There is no way I am listening to your overblown sales pitch."

Mimicking the way he'd looked at her as she'd shimmied her way out of the cake, Lacey let her eyes drift over him slowly and rapaciously, cataloging every ruggedly handsome inch of Lilah and John McCabe's third-born son. He was Texas tall—she guessed about six foot three—and fit. "A little too late for that attitude, isn't it, cowboy, seeing as how you're already tied up and—as it happens—completely at my disposal."

His square jaw shot out pugnaciously. "Now, Dr. Buchanon—"

Lacey shook her head, taking in the mocha-colored suede sportcoat, white open-collared Western shirt and dark denim jeans that fit his well-honed body like a glove. "Hear me out," she told him stubbornly.

The soles of his handcrafted leather boots dug into the scuffed wooden floor beneath him. "I already know what you have to say, and I will never agree." He pushed the words through a row of white, even teeth. "I already have a job."

Lacey studied the thick, velvety brown lashes framing his light sea-blue eyes. "With a prestigious, surgical group practice in Fort Worth. I know."

Jackson McCabe's sensual lips curled up contemptuously. "Then why are you bugging me?" he demanded.

Lacey hiked the fringed hem of her dress a little lower on her thighs and crossed her legs in front of her gracefully. "Because you haven't started there yet— you won't for another month—and we need you here more," she explained rationally.

Tension chiseled the lines of his handsome face into an even more rugged visage. "Sorry," he told her grimly. "Laramie isn't for me."

Lacey did her best to contain her own frustration. Honestly, she'd never met a more mulish, narrow-minded man in her life. "How can you say that?" she demanded, with a great deal more serenity than she felt. He was throwing away his chance to live—and practice medicine—in the paradise of a small, close-knit west Texas community. "You grew up here."

"Precisely. Laramie's a nice place to hail from, but I'm not spending my entire life here."

"You wouldn't be," Lacey rebutted smoothly, doing her level best to persuade him around to her way of thinking. "The way I calculate it"—her voice dropped a soothing notch—"with college in Austin, medical school in Houston, and your residency in Dallas, you've already lived a good thirteen years away from here. That's over one-third of your life."

"Right." Jackson nodded firmly, a lock of his bittersweet chocolate hair falling over his forehead. "And now I'm going to settle in Forth Worth."

Lacey's eyes gleamed. "Not if your family and I have anything to do with it."

Jackson scowled. He should have known his meddling family had a hand in this. No doubt a very big part. Having already managed to discreetly free one hand, he narrowed his eyes at her tousled mane of honey-blond hair and demanded grimly, "Who put you up to this?"

Lacey's green eyes shimmered with mock indignation. "I'll have you know I thought of it all by myself. Of course," she amended with grating playfulness as she tilted her head to one side, "it wouldn't have been necessary had you returned even one of my phone calls or letters over the past three months, Dr. McCabe."

Jackson gritted his teeth as he continued to work on the restraining loops of rope. "I called you back once," he reminded her defiantly.

"But you didn't talk to me directly," Lacey complained. "You talked to my secretary, over at the hospital."

In fact, Jackson recalled, he had insisted on not talking to her directly for just this very reason, because he didn't want it to become a long and involved discussion that was also inherently personal and revealing.

"Right," Jackson concurred dryly. "And when I did I left a very explicit message—that I wasn't interested and you needed to look elsewhere to fill your position."

"I have." Lacey's eyes glowed with a determined light. "No one fits the bill the way you do. Besides, you have family here." She lifted her slender shoulders in an elegant shrug. "I'd think you'd want to be back here."

"Then you're wrong." Jackson had but half a wrist to go. Once both hands were free, he'd be out of this dang chair in no time. "Now admit it and give it up."

Lacey's chin thrust out pugnaciously. "Not until you agree to at least take a look at the newly outfitted surgery suite at Laramie Community Hospital."

Jackson continued surreptitiously inching his trapped wrist out from the ropes even as he gave her a murderous look in response.

"Not gonna do it, huh?" Lacey shrugged. "Well, okay. Suit yourself. I've got all night if you'd—"

Without warning the door burst open, and all three of Jackson's brothers appeared in the doorway. Caught thus, it was all Jackson could do not to groan. "So how's it going in here?" Wade McCabe walked in with the confidence of a self-made millionaire.

"Did she talk you into it yet?" Shane McCabe followed, spurs jingling.

Travis—the oldest—grinned and stroked his jaw. He winked at Shane and Wade. "Looks like he's all tied up to me."

"Very funny, guys." Jackson tried but could not quite get the rest of his wrist free. "Now one of you untie me," he demanded cantankerously.

"Sorry, pardner. Can't do that." Wade shook his head, laughter in his eyes.

"Nope, we sure can't." Shane sighed. "We promised Mom this is one instance where we'd definitely let nature take its course."

Jackson blinked. "Our mother was in on this, too?" he echoed, incredulous.

Wade nodded. "She figured someone needed to talk some sense into you before you made the mistake of moving to Fort Worth permanently. And who better than a pretty girl who also happens to be a doc?"

"Mom wants you home, Jackson," Shane added helpfully.

"Mom is just going to have to get used to it," Jackson grumbled. Even though Lacey Buchanon was sexy as could be, and the most intriguing woman he'd met in ages, she wasn't reason enough to stay—and neither was his family, as much as he loved them. His irritability increasing by leaps and bounds, he turned back to his brothers. "I have my own life now." Jackson glared at Travis—the most serious of his brothers—accusingly. "I can't believe you're in on this, too."

Travis shrugged his broad shoulders carelessly. "We

need a surgeon here, Jackson. And a good one. Like it or not, you're the sawbones everyone wants."

"Based on what?" Jackson said irritably as he regarded his three brothers with misgiving and continued to surreptitiously untie the knot that held him.

"Your golden-boy status in the community, that's what," Shane said, a bit enviously. He leaned over and dropped Jackson's stone-colored Stetson, which he had retrieved from the bar, on the desk. "Everyone knows how good you are with a scalpel, Jackson."

Wade nodded. "They know there's not a finer surgeon in all Texas."

"The bottom line is the people here need you as much as your family does," Travis said gently.

Lacey looked at him, smug contentment in her face. "Sounds to me like you're outnumbered," she stated silkily, her green eyes glowing with a challenging, sassy light. "So what's it gonna be, Jackson. Are you going over to the hospital with me tomorrow?" She leaned over him seductively. "Or are you gonna stay tied up here all night?"

Jackson looked at Lacey and his brothers for a long moment. Without warning, all the fire left his fight. "I'll go." Stunning them all, he abruptly freed his hands from the confining ropes and eased himself out of the chair. "But it'll have to be tonight." Retrieving his hat, he swept a hand through the rumpled layers of his dark brown hair and put it on his head, drawing it low across his brow.

Lacey frowned. She looked uneasy again.

"Don't you want to stay for the rest of the bachelor

party?" she asked, backing up one step and then another.

Turning the tables on Lacey, Jackson let his glance slide lazily over her, checking her—and her sumptuous curves—out in a way he knew darn well irritated the heck out of her. Already heading for the door, he put his hand on her spine, taking her along with him, as he remarked drolly, "Let's just say it's lost its charm for me."

Lacey dug in the heels of her white leather cowgirl boots as they reached the portal. "I can trust you, can't I?"

Jackson lifted both hands and spread them wide. "I'm nothing if not a man of my word," he vowed expansively.

Shane nodded. "If he says he'll go with you over to the hospital, he'll go."

Travis and Wade wordlessly concurred.

"Okay." Lacey drew a deep breath, still looking a little uneasy at Jackson's sudden, unexpected cooperation with her.

Jackson put his hand on the back of her waist, liking the way it felt there. He guided her the rest of the way through the doorway. "Let's go." Then he turned back and rounded on his brothers. "I'll deal with y'all later," he promised.

The three McCabes guffawed as if looking forward to it. Lacey and Jackson headed out the back. Jackson intended to take her to his car, but Lacey stopped in front of an old-fashioned, pink girl's bike, with a flowered white wicker basket attached to the handlebars, that had been propped against the alley wall. "I suppose you've got your car."

"You guessed it."

"Then I'll meet you over there."

Jackson put a staying hand on her wrist. Her skin felt warm and silky beneath his hand. "You're going to ride your bike over there?"

"Sure," Lacey's pulse quickened as she tilted her face up to his. "Why not?"

Jackson told himself her personal safety was none of his business, then found himself saying, anyway, "It's almost midnight."

Lacey shrugged. "The hospital is three blocks from here. And crime in Laramie is nonexistent. It's not Houston or Dallas or even Fort Worth. I'll be perfectly fine."

Jackson knew that. Even so, he didn't like the idea of her running around alone at night. "How are you going to get home?" he demanded.

Lacey rolled her eyes and used the toe of her boot to lift the kickstand on her bike. "Same way. My apartment is only two blocks from the hospital."

Having no valid argument against that, Jackson asked, "Don't you have a car?"

Lacey regarded him with exasperation. "Of course. I just don't use it unless I need to. There's no use wasting money on gasoline to go short distances when the weather's nice and I need to exercise, anyway. This way—" Lacey lifted one shapely leg and slid over onto the seat of her bike "—I kill two birds with one stone, so to speak."

Jackson planted his hands on his hips and shook his

head. "Well, I don't have time to wait for you to bicycle on over there, so slide your fanny off that seat. You're coming with me."

Lacey gave him a droll look even as her jaw shot out mutinously and the first hint of temper glinted in her eyes. "In a hurry?"

"You could say that." He waited just long enough for her to get off her bike and put the kickstand back down, then took her by the elbow and steered her around front.

Lacey tossed her head. "I'd heard that about you," she muttered disparagingly beneath her breath.

Jackson spared her a glance but kept them both moving. "What?"

"That you weren't one to waste time while you were climbing the ladder of success."

"Then you heard right." He stopped in front of a black Porsche and opened the door via the remote control on his key chain.

As the door swung open, the new-car smell wafted out. Lacey sat down in the leather. "Nice," she admitted.

Jackson shut the door, circled around to the driver side and climbed in behind the wheel. "I think so. It's just one of the perks of my new job in Fort Worth."

Lacey pivoted in her seat, the skirt of her dress hiking up to show another inch of long lissome thigh. "They bought it for you?"

Jackson shook his head and promptly disabused her of that notion.

"It's a lease, paid for courtesy of the group practice," he told her smoothly as he turned the key.

"You have to get back and forth to the hospital and office somehow."

"Exactly," Jackson murmured as the engine purred to life and he eased the sleek car away from the curve.

Lacey let out an enormous sigh and rolled her eyes, settling more comfortably in the sumptuous leather seat.

Jackson shot her a glance and tried not to think how much he liked the flower-and-woman fragrance of her perfume. "You disapprove?"

Lacey settled her own hat lower across her brow. "Let's just say I don't see the value of it."

Jackson didn't care if she did or didn't. "I like nice things," he told her bluntly. He'd worked hard for them, and he'd be damned if he was going to apologize for it.

"Hmm." She made another faintly disapproving sound as the two-story white-stone community hospital came into view. Jackson followed the signs and parked in the doctor's parking lot. Jackson remembered coming here with his parents, who both worked at the hospital, when he was a kid. Initially, it had only had fifteen beds and no real emergency room, but several additions and much tender loving care later, it had one hundred beds and a fully equipped emergency room, as well as office suites for all the doctors practicing in the area.

They walked inside, bypassing the E.R. in favor of the elevators at the end of the soothing mint-green-and-white hallway. "Mind if we stop by to see a new patient of mine before we head up to the O.R.?" Lacey asked, their footsteps echoing on the shiny linoleum floor.

"Not at all." For Jackson, as well as Lacey, the patients always came first. Jackson paused in front of the elevator and waited for the doors to open. When they did, Lacey led the way inside.

"Where do you want me to wait?" Jackson asked as the doors slid shut, closing them in together.

Lacey pushed 2, leaned against the opposite wall and kept her eyes on his. "You can tag along."

"Afraid to let me out of your sight?"

Lacey smiled mysteriously. "Something like that."

The doors opened and they stepped off the elevator into the rainbow-hued color scheme of the pediatrics wing. Stuffed animals and toys, donated by the many charitable organizations in Laramie, decorated the wing. Brightly colored murals of cartoon characters livened up the walls. Standing behind the nurses' station were two nurses in shocking-pink smocks. The younger one—who appeared to be about seven months pregnant—Jackson hadn't met. But he knew the brunette with the lively eyes. Nurse Ada Peterson had not only worked at the hospital for years, she'd made no secret of her disapproval of his plans to settle down permanently and practice medicine elsewhere.

As Lacey and Jackson moved toward them, he heard the younger nurse murmur to Ada, "Well what do you know? Looks like that crazy plan of hers is working after all."

What plan? Jackson wondered with swiftly escalating resentment, taking in Ada Peterson's amused smile.

He shot a glance at Lacey. If she'd heard what Ada had said, she was doing her best to ignore it as she affably greeted the two nurses at the desk and grabbed a chart and a stethoscope. Nurse Peterson did not look the least bit surprised to see Lacey in cowgirl garb as she said happily, "Glad to see you were able to talk young Dr. McCabe into stopping by with you." Which meant, Jackson thought, biting down on a salty oath, everyone at the hospital had known about Lacey's cockeyed plan to snare him for the hospital via his hormones.

The younger nurse—Nancy—nodded, her hand on her swollen tummy.

"It'll be a comfort, knowing he's around in case—" Nancy broke off abruptly as her co-worker elbowed her. "Well." She cleared her throat, watching as Lacey looped the borrowed stethoscope around her neck. "I expect the two of you better go on back."

"That is," Nurse Ada Peterson added, pausing to look Jackson up and down before turning back to Lacey, "if young Dr. McCabe is seeing Molly Weatherby right along with you."

Lacey flushed slightly, and for the first time that evening seemed at a loss for words. Fortunately, Jackson wasn't.

"Oh, I am." Jackson said. As soon as they turned the corner, he swung open the supply room door, took a slight detour and pushed Lacey inside.

"What are you doing?" she demanded in astonishment as he fumbled for the light switch. While it might have been great to nestle against her in the dark, he wanted to see her face while he questioned her.

"What do you think I'm doing?" Jackson growled right back as he planted a hand on either side of her and used his body to flatten her against the wall. "Getting the scoop."

She lifted an inquiring brow. "About what?"

"Molly Weatherby, for starters." Steadfastly ignoring the fluid way her body trembled against his, Jackson leaned in even closer and quizzed her. "What have I got to do with her?"

Lacey shrugged as if their proximity were no big deal and gnawed on her lower lip. "Nothing at the moment," she said with an innocence that was definitely not to be trusted.

Jackson glared at Lacey Buchanon, all too aware this wasn't the first time he'd been bamboozled into unwittingly helping someone else with their hidden agenda, but it sure as hell was going to be the last. There was no way on this earth he was going to let himself be used by a woman again, no matter how valiant or community-minded her plan happened to be. "Is this patient—"

"Molly Weatherby," Lacey provided helpfully.

"—a surgical case?"

Lacey shoved him aside and swept past with a haughty toss of her head. "Right now it's too soon to tell," she told him matter-of-factly. "Now, if you don't mind, I think I should go see her."

Lacey headed for the room without a backward glance, leaving him to follow at will. Figuring he should at least know what this was about, he did.

As the two of them walked into the patient's room, five-year-old Molly Weatherby was settled in the curve of her mother's arm, a storybook in front of them. She was clad in crayon-print hospital pajamas, her short, curly red hair hopelessly mussed and smushed down on one side, her round apple cheeks flushed with fever.

A child-size basin on the table next to her hospital bed, she had an IV taped to the back of her arm and what looked to be a much-loved fuzzy brown teddy bear cradled against her chest and tucked up beneath her chin.

Lacey paused to chuck Molly playfully on the end of her nose and look down at her gently before she stroked the teddy bear's head. "Who's your friend here?" she asked softly.

"Teddy Beddy." Molly cuddled her bear even closer and looked up at Lacey with adoring eyes. "I call him that 'cause I always take him to bed with me."

Lacey grinned. "He sure is cute. I especially like the rainbow stripes on the suspenders of his overalls."

"Me, too." Molly pressed a tender kiss in the top of her teddy bear's head.

"So how come you're still up?" Lacey asked, taking in the cot that had been set up for Patricia in the corner. Clearly, Jackson noted, it had yet to be used. Lacey looked at Molly's mom. "After the harrowing day you two have had, I thought you'd both be asleep by now."

"I keep waking up," Molly explained.

Patricia smoothed her daughter's hair. "I think it's the fever—she's usually restless whenever she has one." Lacey glanced at the chart and noted—as did Jackson—that it was still 102.2.

"How's your tummy feeling? Is it still hurting?" Lacey asked her patient gently.

Molly patted the center of her tummy. "It hurts a little bit right here."

Her expression calm, Lacey handed the chart to Jackson, in lieu of putting it aside. "Let's take a look." Lacey smiled at Molly. "Shall we?"

* * *

Aware Jackson was standing to the left of her, watching her every move, Lacey palpated Molly's abdomen. As before, there was no abdominal muscle spasm or resistance in the abdomen. Lacey pressed her stethoscope to Molly's tummy. "What about the nausea?" she asked, noting the sounds were moderately active.

Molly made a face. "I still feel a little yucky."

"But the medicine and IV fluids have already helped a lot in that regard," Patricia volunteered happily. "She hasn't been sick to her tummy for several hours now."

"But my mommy's staying right here with me." Molly announced, as she cuddled against her mother, "Just in case."

"That's good to hear on both counts." Lacey grinned.

"Do you know yet whether it's the stomach flu or appendicitis?" Patricia Weatherby asked worriedly.

"We don't have an absolute diagnosis just yet," Lacey said honestly, then went on to explain. "Usually with appendicitis along with the nausea, vomiting and the elevated temperature Molly's already experiencing, there's localized tenderness in the midepigastrium or right lower quadrant, and an elevated white cell count. At this point Molly has neither of those last two symptoms."

"So it could just be a severe case of the stomach flu, made worse by the fact we were in the middle of a cross-country move and traveling by car when it hit," Patricia Weatherby theorized anxiously.

Of the two alternatives, it was definitely the one

to hope for, Lacey thought. "It's entirely possible, although not ironclad at this point, which is why we want to keep Molly here for evaluation at least another day or so. Sometimes a disease must run its natural course for the diagnosis to become apparent. But we should know more as things develop in the next day or so."

Patricia began to look worried again. "Meaning she'll get better quickly if it's the stomach flu and won't if it's appendicitis," she guessed slowly.

Lacey nodded. "Right." Only time would tell.

"Then I vote for it being the stomach flu," Patricia said.

"Me, too," Molly said as she studied Lacey's short, fringed dress, boots and the hat she'd let slide down her back on its string. "Were you at a party?" she asked curiously.

"As a matter of fact, I was."

Molly shyly fingered the cover of her storybook. "I like your dress. It's pretty."

Lacey smiled. "Thanks."

Molly pointed to Jackson, her curiosity unabated. "Who's he?"

Lacey turned to Jackson and waved him forward. "This is Dr. Jackson McCabe. Not to be confused with his father, Dr. John McCabe, who's been on staff here at the hospital for many years."

"Father and son, both doctors! How nice!" Patricia Weatherby enthused as she stretched out her hand. "We're pleased to meet you."

Jackson smiled and shook hands with her graciously. "Likewise."

"I'll be back to see you in the morning, okay?" Outside in the hall, Lacey turned to Jackson. She noted uncomfortably that he didn't look all that pleased at being given the lowdown, however inadvertently, on a possible surgical case, but she'd be darned if she'd apologize for it. She had a five-year-old patient to look out for, and like it or not, Jackson was the only surgeon—albeit a vacationing one—in a forty-five-mile radius. If the hospital had any kind of surgical emergency while he was here, he was likely to be drafted into helping out whether he liked it or not.

Meanwhile, Lacey thought, she'd just hope for the best and play it cool. "Thanks for just hanging out while I talked to Molly." Lacey headed for the nurses' station, where she dropped off both the chart and the stethoscope and filled the nurses in on her findings.

"You'll pay me back for my patience and understanding, I'm sure," Jackson told her the moment they continued on.

Deliberately ignoring the come-hither note in his low tone, Lacey stiffened her spine and hurried down the hall. She led him around the corner, through the double swinging doors and into the adjacent wing, her demeanor professional and efficient. "You'll be surprised at what we've done to the operating suite," she told him expansively. She knew the tile and flooring were the same, but the equipment, from the operating table to the television monitors and lasers were all as new and state of the art as the hospital could afford. Jackson looked around with admiration. "This operating room must have cost the hospital a pretty penny."

Lacey nodded proudly. "We all knew we needed to

update it," she explained. "It was just a matter of raising the funds for it."

Jackson opened the supply cabinet, poked around a bit and finally withdrew a roll of surgical tape. "Unfortunately, it's still the only operating room in the hospital."

Lacey shrugged and hopped up on the end of the table, crossing her legs at the knee. "It's all we need right now since we only have one surgeon on staff."

Jackson prowled closer. Lifting one hand, he stroked it down her face and looked at her regretfully. "It's still not going to work." Dropping his hand, he turned away from her and continued messing with the tape. "You're not going to get me emotionally involved here, no matter how many patients you drag me to see."

Lacey regarded him confidently. "A girl can dream," she teased.

"No," Jackson said as he set the tape down on the table next to her. "You can't." He took her in his arms and guided her backward. The next thing Lacey knew she was lying prone on the operating table and both her hands were caught in one of his.

"What are you doing now?" she asked in the most bored tone she could manage as he shifted her hands above her head and held them there.

"You tied me to a chair." With his free hand, he picked up the roll of surgical tape. "Now—" he tore off a strip with his teeth "—I'm taping you to a table."

Lacey knew she could easily break free of him, but she refused to dignify his outrageous behavior with a struggle. She let a smile tug at her lips for several seconds before she gave in to it. "This is not exactly original, cowboy."

"True. On the other hand," he paused to tape her wrists to the table, "turnabout is fair play."

It took every bit of self-control Lacey had to remain still—and smiling. "Okay, cowboy, fun's over." Still smiling, she looked him straight in the eye. "Now let me go."

His gaze still squarely on hers, he slowly shook his head and leaned closer still. "Not until you promise to stop bugging me about taking a position here," he said softly but firmly.

"I haven't bugged you at all!" Lacey exclaimed in heated self-defense. *Yet.*

Jackson sat down next to her and let out a snort of disbelief. "I see. And what would you call jumping out of a cake at my dad's party and tying me up to get my attention? Not to mention inviting me over here, taking me to see a patient of yours who just might be needing surgery in the next few days and bringing me up here to the newly outfitted O.R.?" Jackson demanded.

Lacey shrugged and moved her wrists as much as the tape would allow. Damn but he had taped her down well. "Good politics?" she ventured lightly, and hoped he had not noticed how much her pulse had picked up since the edge of his hip had started nudging the edge of hers.

Jackson grimaced. "I call it a waste of time." Planting a hand on either side of her, he leaned so close she could feel his body heat. "Now I want your promise before I let you go," he said sternly. "From this point forward, no more pressuring me. No more talk of me going into private practice here."

It had always been Lacey's policy to never promise anything she couldn't deliver on. "Sorry," Lacey reported fliply, refusing to give in to his demands. "No can do." Not, she thought determinedly, when Laramie needed a surgeon so badly.

Jackson's dark brows lowered like twin thunderclouds over his eyes. "Then you're not getting out of here," he said flatly.

Deciding abruptly he wasn't the only one who'd had enough, Lacey struggled uselessly against the tape, wiggling this way and that. "The heck I'm not!" she fumed. Whether he liked it or not, this particular game was over!

Jackson watched, arms crossed nonchalantly in front of him. "I don't care how fit you are. You can't possibly break through that tape, so you might as well stop trying."

Lacey stopped wiggling and drew a deep breath as they continued to size each other up. "You know, on second thought, you're right. I won't have to. I'll just scream for help and half the staff will come running!"

He shook his head and leaned even closer, not stopping till their bodies were but an inch apart. "I don't think so."

She shot him a dark, warning glance and retorted grimly, "Watch me."

"No, Lacey," Jackson said as he swiftly took her into his arms again, taped wrists and all. "You watch me."

Chapter 2

Jackson hadn't counted on a kiss figuring anywhere into this, but damned if he wasn't enjoying the soft warmth of her lips surrendering to his. Lacey kissed the way she had danced on top of the bar, with fire and passion and an all-consuming zest for life. Which was, Jackson schooled himself, precisely why he needed to call a halt now. She was too soft and too close, too warmly accessible. Much more of this and he'd forget why he'd started such a foolish proposition in the first place. As abruptly as he'd taken her in his arms, he released her.

Lacey blinked and shook herself back into the present. She shot him an indignant look. "What was that for?" she demanded.

Jackson shrugged as if the potent kiss had hardly mattered—another lie, it had!—and tore his gaze from the dewy softness of her just-kissed lips. "To shut you up. You were fixing to scream for help, remember?"

"I remember." Deep pink color swept across her face. "And as far as putting the muzzle on me, it didn't work."

But it had done *something,* Jackson thought wryly as his fingers brushed down her face, stroked along her jaw. It had shown them both just how hot and sexy the chemistry between them was, and now that they knew, well, he imagined it would be a cold day in Hades before either one of them forgot.

"So what are you saying?" he teased. Her skin was soft as silk and she was trembling, the pulse at the base of her neck fluttering wildly. "That you're still planning to kick up a ruckus so someone will come to your rescue?"

Lacey regarded him irately. "That, cowboy, is exactly what I'm saying."

Mercy. The woman knew how to bait him into doing what they both wanted. "Then I guess…" he drawled, not surprised he was already hungry for the taste and feel of her again. Sifting his hands through her hair, he lowered his head, tilted his head slightly to the right, and moved in even closer. "I'll just have to do it again."

Lacey moaned as he invaded her warm, wet mouth with his tongue.

Heavens above, this cowboy knew how to kiss. Knew just how to tease and distract and caress and leave her hot and aching and wanting more. But she wasn't going to give in to him, she decided resolutely, even as she melted against him all the more. She wasn't going to let him scare her into staying away from him—and his sexy advances—while he was in town. She had a job to do. A mission. She had been appointed the person in charge of recruiting a surgeon for Laramie Community Hospital and by golly that was exactly what she was going to do—no matter how many obstacles he put in front of her.

With that in mind she stiffened against him. He lifted his head. Her temper soaring as surely as her libido, Lacey looked up at him defiantly and smiled like the fiercely independent woman she was. "Cute, cowboy," she said, pretending neither kiss had affected her in the slightest, when she knew full well they'd wreaked absolute havoc on her senses. "Too bad you aren't intimidating me one bit," she told him.

Jackson looked her in the eye, not the least bit deterred. "You know what they say—" he took her chin in hand and held it so she had nowhere to look but his eyes "—the third time is the charm."

If the first two kisses had been incredible in their effectiveness and intensity, the third was absolutely devastating. His lips gently met hers, at first just softly exploring, hinting at the passion he was holding back. Mere sex, she could have fought. And won. But this, Lacey sighed, as wistfulness swept through her body with debilitating speed. This seduction of heart and will and soul, this sure and tender cosseting of her body, left her helpless and vulnerable and wanting more. It left her wanting to see where this would lead.

What the heck, she might as well roll with the punches, she decided, giving in to the moment, the man, and surged against him. Slowly, but surely, the pressure of his lips grew more possessive, and somehow that made the culmination of their desire all the sweeter. The hardness of his chest pressed against the softness of her breasts until she could feel his heartbeat marking time with her own. Never had she imagined such desire, she thought dizzily as his tongue dipped and swirled, nuzzled, savored—seduced! Never had she imagined she'd be locked in his arms, her heart pounding, her head swimming, her spirits soaring, a mere hour or so after meeting him. But she was, and she hardly knew what to do about it.

It was that moment—when she would have surrendered all to him—that he lifted his head and traced the dewy softness of her lower lip with the pad of his thumb. "What?" he prodded softly, abruptly looking as besotted as she felt. "No smart retort this time?"

Smart retorts had brought her nothing but more kisses, Lacey thought, pushing the remainder of her vulnerable feelings away. She remained mutinously silent, glaring at him, while she did what she should have done from the outset and began working her wrists from the tape.

His dark brows drew together in exaggerated perplexity as he began to help her free herself. "You have nothing at all to say?"

More silence as she she pursed her lips together and looked down her nose at him.

"Fortunately you can still nod." Ever so gently he helped her remove the rest of the tape. "So promise me you'll stop badgering me about the job."

"Fine." Lacey swung her legs over the edge of the table and, sat up. Flattening a hand on the solid wall of his chest, she shoved him aside. She jumped down from the table and strode—albeit a little wobbily—toward the door. "I will never again suggest you take the staff position here." Haughtily, flinging the hair from her face she tossed a parting shot over her shoulder. "You're not cut out for it, anyway."

Now that rankled, Jackson thought. Not about to let her get away with it, he lengthened his strides and cut in front of her. "What did you say?"

A provoking smile on her face, Lacey folded her arms in front of her chest and squared off with him deliberately. "You haven't got the guts."

Jackson quirked a brow. "Excuse me?"

Lacey lifted her elegant shoulders in indifference. "Why practice here with limited resources when you can go to Fort Worth and have every piece of dream equipment, not to mention boundless state-of-the-art surgical suites, available to you?"

Finally, she understood. "Exactly."

"Whereas here," Lacey continued baiting him with a silky look that upped his still-racing pulse another notch, "you'd have to rely on your wits and skill. Here you'd have to do so much with so little. Obviously, Jackson," she purred with a ready smile that challenged him even more, "you're not up for the task."

The hell I'm not, Jackson thought, his own temper beginning to burn. Nevertheless, he was not falling into her trap. He was not going to let her make him feel guilty, dammit!

Rolling his weight onto his toes, he towered over her and said softly, "If you're waiting for me to argue with you, you're going to turn old and gray."

To Jackson's consternation, Lacey merely smiled

as if she couldn't have cared less what he did, and shrugged again. "See you around, Jackson," she murmured lightly.

He watched her leave, muttering just loudly enough to make sure she heard, "Not if I see you first."

As Lacey suspected, her mother was waiting up for her in the apartment above the bakery. "So how'd it go?" Isabel Buchanon asked, her trim petite form, pretty heart-shaped face and neatly curled pale blond hair showing none of the heartache she'd been through in her life.

Lacey tossed off her cowgirl hat, kicked off her boots, and settled onto the cozy chintz sofa, letting the bone-deep weariness overtake her. "Better and worse than you could ever imagine."

Isabel shook her head as she tightened the belt on her fluffy, pink chenille robe and disappeared into the adjacent galley kitchen. "I can't believe you actually jumped out of that cake!"

Lacey shrugged, knowing, even if her mother didn't, it had been no big deal. "The McCabe boys wanted a stripper to surprise their dad, and where were they gonna find one in Laramie? Besides the whole thing was G-rated. I didn't show any more of myself than I do at the swimming pool."

Isabel brought two glasses of milk over to the coffee table then returned to get a plate of freshly baked cookies. "Doc must've been surprised," she said, seating herself.

Lacey picked up a delicious oatmeal cookie chock-full of apples, raisins, walnuts and chocolate chips.

"Not as much as his doctor son," she murmured, her thoughts going unwillingly back to the very sexy kisses she and Jackson McCabe had shared in the O.R. One thing you could say about Jackson, he certainly wasn't shy when it came to getting what he wanted, which had been—at least for a few minutes, there—her.

Isabel sipped her milk. "Were you able to talk Jackson into staying in Laramie?"

Lacey demolished one cookie and reached for another. "He thinks I'm one brick shy of a load to even bring the subject up," she told her mother.

"But you persisted, anyway."

Through a lot of kisses, heck yes, I persisted. Lacey regarded her mother seriously. "I had to, Mom. Laramie Community Hospital needs a surgeon. Because he was brought up here, still has family in the area and is reputedly immensely talented in his field, Jackson McCabe is the logical choice, as well as the one everyone wants."

"But he doesn't think so," Isabel guessed.

Lacey set her jaw. "He will."

Isabel's eyes sparkled with maternal affection and an inherent knowledge of Lacey's heart that Lacey sometimes wished wasn't so laser-accurate. "What makes you so sure?" Isabel asked.

Those kisses. Damn, but they'd been hot!

Lacey pushed the unbidden thought aside. Jackson McCabe was not going to stay in the area because of her, no matter how hot or real the chemistry between them, and it was ridiculous to entertain such an idea, even in fantasy. He might, however, stay because of his family and the legacy of service his mother and father were leaving at this very hospital. Aware her mother was waiting for an answer to her question, Lacey drew a deep breath and replied, "Hope. Raw hope."

Isabel tried, but wasn't quite able to suppress a sigh. "I'd hate to see you be disappointed," she said gently.

Lacey pushed her own uneasiness away. She wasn't going to get involved with the wrong man again, no matter how devastatingly handsome, or hard to get, or sexy he was. She'd already done so once, to disastrous results. "I won't be." She drained the last of the milk and, not wanting to think about Jackson McCabe or her unprecedented, sensual reaction to him again, pushed to her feet. Leaning down, she kissed her mother's brow and hugged her gently. "I'm not the only one with an early call. Better get to bed."

Several miles away, Jackson walked into the ranch house where he had grown up. His dad was nowhere in sight, but his three brothers were still up, doing what they loved to do best when they were anywhere near Lilah McCabe's incredibly delicious home cooking— raiding the fridge and pantry.

As expected, his brothers wasted no time at all ribbing him even as they delved into the facts. "Sure took you long enough to get home," his brother Shane drawled with a lascivious wink, reminding Jackson why, at age thirty, Shane was considered the wildest son, footloose and fancy-free. And although Shane had once sworn it would be a cold day in hell before he ever settled down, and gave up being a rodeo cowboy— he'd been one of the most successful ones in the entire country—he was now going to use his winnings to start up a horse ranch of his own.

"So how was she?" Shane demanded impatiently.

In a word, *fantastic*, Jackson thought as he pulled up a chair and joined his brothers at the big oak kitchen table where they'd studied and fought and eaten and done their homework for years. "How was who?" Jackson asked with deliberate stupidity as he helped himself to a piece of the pecan pie his brothers were demolishing, and ate the rich confection right from his hand.

"You know who we mean." Shane tossed him the can of real whipped cream. "The stripper."

Jackson squirted a generous dollop of whipped cream onto the center of his pie. "I wouldn't know." He continued munching on his pie laconically. "After we finished at the hospital, I dropped her back at the bar and she bicycled home."

Travis, the oldest and most responsible of all the McCabe sons, and the only one of them to take up cattle ranching, quirked a disapproving brow. "You let a lady take *herself* home at this time of night?" he asked, stunned.

Hell, no, Jackson thought irritably to himself. He had followed her in his Porsche, and waited while she let herself in to the front door of her mother's bakeshop. But Jackson figured there was no reason his brothers needed to know that, so he concentrated on other things instead, like the way she grated on him like nobody's business.

"Lacey Buchanon's no lady, she's a do-gooding

busybody who needs to learn to mind her own business."

His brother Wade, a multimillionaire businessman-investor who liked his risks to pan out whether in romance or any other arena, regarded Jackson with the usual combination of big-brother protectiveness and calculation. "She's also a damn fine pediatrician, from what Mom and Dad say."

Jackson took another mouthful of his mother's prize-winning pie. "She needs to keep her opinions to herself."

Shane slapped his knee. "So she *did* get under his skin. Told you boys she would. The minute I saw her come shimmying out of the top of that cake—" Shane shook his head in wistful remembrance "—I knew she was one fun-lovin' gal."

Jackson glared at his younger brother. The last thing he wanted was Shane making a pass at Lacey, too. "Knock it off, would you?"

Travis spoke up. "Leave him alone, fellas. His love life—or lack of it—is his own."

"Amen to that," Jackson agreed, getting up to pour himself a tall glass of icy cold milk.

"I guess you're right," Wade agreed with a calculated wink as he helped himself to a second piece of pie. "Besides," Wade, who was no slouch in the romance department himself, teased, "anyone can see he's got the hots for her."

Jackson glared at Wade. What was it about coming home to his three brothers that had him feeling—and acting—like a fifteen-year-old again? It was just this

nosy interference that had made him look elsewhere—
anywhere else—for a job in the first place.

That and the fact he'd never be known here as anything but the son of the real Doc McCabe.

"The question is, were the hots returned?" Shane
teased.

Jackson scowled as his temper—usually in such
cool control—burned all the hotter. "How'd you like
a knuckle sandwich to go with that pie?" he asked his
brother Shane, pushing back his chair. He was not
going to allow Lacey's reputation to be impugned as
a result of being with him. If she wanted to ruin that,
she could ruin it on her own!

"Boys!" a soft melodic voice sounded behind him.

The four of them turned in unison to see a gentle
woman, standing there in her bathrobe and slippers.
Her blond hair was threaded with gray these days, but
her eyes were as blue and lively as ever. She regarded
them all sternly, her hands on her hips. "Y'all behave
now, you hear me?"

Jackson and his brothers exchanged a glance, knowing full well that when they were together—which
wasn't often enough these days now that they were all
grown-up and leading lives of their own—they never
could resist raising a little hell. Nor could Lilah resist
slipping back into her role of family matriarch and
pulling them instantly—and good-humoredly, back
in line.

"Yes ma'am," they echoed in unison, the four of
them doing their level best not to smile or let their
mother know how much they loved coming back to

her this way and, just for a moment, slipping into the safety and the security that had been their childhood.

"Your father's asleep," Lilah continued, lifting a brow at the two empty pie plates in the center of the table, "and I don't want any of you to wake him."

"No ma'am."

She padded into the kitchen and, eyes twinkling happily at the sight of her four boys gathered at her kitchen table, set about making herself some tea. "It's nice to have you boys all home, even if it is only briefly. What would be even nicer," Lilah added sweetly, "is if you had wives and children along with you to attend the renewal of your father's and my wedding vows."

A collective groan swept through the group. "Don't start," Shane said, as always the first to roll his eyes. "I'm not anywhere near ready to settle down."

"Me either," Wade concurred, pushing back his chair.

"I'm too busy to worry about a wife," Travis stated flatly, crossing his arms in front of him.

"And I—" Jackson announced loftily, determined to make no secret of the fact "—am looking to have a little fun, now that I'm finally out of med school and have finished my residency."

Lilah studied Jackson. "You can have fun with the right woman," Lilah said.

The right woman. Jackson suspected that was true. He also had an idea from the way everyone was looking at him that his mother and brothers had suddenly decided who the right woman was. He put up a staying hand. "Don't even think it, any of you," he warned.

"Think what?" his mother asked, all innocence, as she laid a hand across her heart.

Jackson scowled. "You are not pairing me up with her and that's final!"

Like the rest of his brothers, Jackson hauled his gear upstairs to his room and spent the night in the bed he'd slept in as a kid. He twisted and turned in an effort to get comfortable on the thirty-year-old mattress, to no avail. For starters, he was just too damn tall to be comfortable in a regulation twin bed these days. And second, he just couldn't seem to stop dreaming about a beautiful woman jumping out of a cake, leading him astray, lassoing him to a chair, and kissing him back like there was no tomorrow.

As a result, he woke tired and cranky, and regretting the fact they'd stopped at just the kisses. More annoying still was the fact his back wasn't the only part of his anatomy that was aching.

Grimacing, Jackson headed for a long cold shower, then sauntered downstairs to join his brothers and parents for that rare meal together in the McCabe ranch house.

"Hey there, Sleeping Beauty, glad you could join us," Jackson's dad teased, as Jackson helped himself to a mug of steaming coffee and then pulled up a chair at the large table in the center of the country kitchen.

"You're just in time to go through these." Lilah stopped flipping pancakes long enough to set a stack of envelopes down in front of Jackson.

Jackson scanned them warily. "What's all this?"

"Exactly what it looks like," Lilah told him cheerfully. "Invitations."

Jackson continued to regard them as if they were a coiled snake, ready to strike. "To what?"

Lilah took one batch of pancakes off the griddle and poured more. "Just about everything, I'd say."

Jackson did a rough estimation and figured the tally was in the double digits and then some. "I can't go to all these. I'm only going to be here a month!"

Lilah set a heaping plate of pancakes and bacon in front of her son. "Sure you can. They're all scheduled on different days, at different times. None of the events overlap by even an hour."

Jackson bypassed the butter and reached for the syrup, making no effort to hide his reluctance. "How did that happen?"

For the first time, Lilah's smile faltered slightly. "How do you think?" Shane said with a meaningful look.

Jackson swore silently to himself and dropped his head. He let out a low groan. "Not Margaret, please." Not Margaret, the bane of his youth.

Wade said with a grin, "She's just making sure every gal in town gets a turn to woo you."

Jackson glared at his brothers. "This isn't funny."

"Speak for yourself. We—" Shane encompassed his other two brothers with a sweeping glance "—find it darn amusing."

Jackson glared at them one by one. The only thing in front of each of them was a plateful of pancakes. "I don't see any of you with invitations."

"That's because we're not *the* eligible bachelor of all Laramie," Travis pointed out mildly. "You are."

"How did I get the honor?" Jackson grumbled.

"Simple," Travis explained as if speaking to the village idiot. "You're a doctor, fresh out of his residency, who should be looking to settle down. At least that's the way the ladies feel. You being so busy and all, doctoring folks, it only follows you'd need a wife to darn your socks for you. So now you got the local ladies standing in line waiting to do just that."

Jackson scowled and took another bite of bacon. His brothers were getting way too much amusement out of this. "If my socks get holes in them, I'll toss 'em out and buy new ones. And, anyway, what's wrong with Wade, if these women are looking for someone to marry? Wade's a multimillionaire."

Shane passed his empty plate to Lilah for seconds. "All the women around here know he only chases society babes."

"And business deals," Travis added helpfully.

Wade lifted his hands as if to say, What can you do? "It's true—I like my ladies in silks and satins, and heaven knows you won't find that around Laramie on a regular basis."

"Okay, so you're out, as far as the local husband hunters are concerned," Jackson interrupted curtly. He turned to the oldest of the four McCabe sons. "What about Travis?"

Travis smiled and helped himself to more coffee. "I'm married to my ranch," he quipped.

Guffaws echoed all around. Jackson only wished he could be thusly amused.

"The ladies also know Travis is too busy rescuing women to bed 'em," Shane added.

It was Travis's turn to frown. "Look, I don't take advantage of a woman, okay? Not ever," he said flatly.

"How very noble," Jackson muttered. He turned to Shane. "That still leaves you."

Shane shrugged and flashed a lazy grin. "They all think I'm a rodeo bum."

"But we know different," Jackson shot back, aiming a thumb at his brother's chest. "That you've saved all your prize money and are now looking to buy some land and start up a horse ranch of your own right this very minute. You just haven't decided where yet."

"Of course," Lilah interjected, as she refilled her own coffee cup and joined them at the table, "your father and I hope it will be somewhere close, Shane."

For the first time Shane looked like he was on a hot seat. "It'll be somewhere in Texas, but that's all I can promise."

The grandfather clock in the foyer chimed, alerting them to the time. Wade pushed his chair back and carried his empty plate over to the dishwasher. "Thanks for breakfast, Mom." Wade took one last gulp of coffee, then turned and looked at Shane. "If you want to hitch a ride back to Houston with me on my chopper, better get your gear together now."

Shane nodded toward the bags standing next to the back door. "I'm way ahead of you, brother."

Travis stood, too. "Guess I better get a move on, too, if I want to get all my ranch chores done today." He wrapped an arm about Lilah's shoulders and kissed his mother's cheek. "Best meal I've had in ages."

Lilah smiled. "Come by more often."

A flurry of thanks and goodbyes followed. Finally Jackson was left with his parents. "What are you off to today?" he asked, aware for the first time in weeks and weeks he didn't have a specific agenda of his own to fulfill.

"Hospital, as always," Lilah said. "Your father is going to try to put a dent in clearing out his office this morning, then work on the seminar about rural medicine we're giving later in the week. I've got to work a full shift and pull together the work schedule for the nursing staff for the entire summer—which won't be easy, considering how many vacations there are going to be—it seems everyone wants off over the July Fourth holiday."

Jackson lifted a brow. "I thought you were retiring, too, Mom."

"Not until your father and I repeat our wedding vows in four weeks." Lilah busied herself wiping down the stove. "Until then, I'll continue as the nursing supervisor for Laramie Community Hospital."

Jackson kicked back in his chair. "Any idea who will replace you yet?" he asked curiously, knowing it would have to be someone first-rate. Laramie Community Hospital might be small, it might be located in the country, but they still hired only the best.

Lilah smiled. "We've already arranged for one of the Lockhart girls—Meg—to replace me."

"Did she ever get married?"

"No." Lilah looked a little troubled. "Nor has she ever told anyone, including her family, who fathered her five-year-old son."

Jackson recalled full well what a scandal it had been when Meg—the responsible one of the four sisters—became pregnant during her last year of nursing school. "What has she told the little boy?" he asked quietly.

"Nothing substantial—yet. But you know that can't go on." Lilah and John exchanged glances before Lilah went on worriedly, "The older he gets the more questions he's going to ask."

"She's going to have to tell him something about his paternity," John agreed.

"That may be one of the reasons she wants to move back to Laramie," Lilah said quietly. "She probably figures it'll be easier for him to hear whatever it is here, when he's surrounded by family."

Jackson's brow furrowed. "I thought just Jenna was living here now."

"At the moment, but Kelsey and Dani are moving back, too."

John grinned, recalling no doubt what a handful the Lockhart girls had been growing up. "'Bout time we had some Lockhart women here again."

Jackson had to admit if ever there had been an answer to the McCabe men it was the Lockhart women—there was nothing and no one the feisty bunch couldn't take on. At least in their view, he amended silently.

"In the meantime—" Lilah picked up the stack of messages and handed them over "—I am not your social director, Jackson," she informed him sternly. "So start calling these women back, and let them know if you are planning to be at these events or not."

* * *

"You don't have to spend your vacation helping me move out of my office," John McCabe said.

Jackson grinned. "No offense, Dad, but after thirty years in one office suite, you've accumulated quite a lot of stuff." In fact, the office was stuffed with presents from patients, memorabilia from all four of his sons as they grew up, not to mention countless medical and community awards.

John shook his head as he looked at the four boxes they had already filled. And they'd barely made a dent in the task. "Your mother said it would take me days to clear all this out. She was right."

Jackson shrugged. Unlike his parents, he didn't see what the hurry was, since his dad wasn't going to officially stop practicing medicine here for another four weeks. "You could just wait until after your last day of work here, move it all back to the ranch house and then sort it out."

"Ah, there's the rub. Your mother said no way am I moving all this stuff from here to there in one truck-load. I have to sort first, decide what I want to keep, and then send only the important stuff back to the ranch. Besides, as soon as we finish here at the hospital and say our vows, we're packing up and taking off for an extended second honeymoon. Whoever takes over in my place here as head of the family medicine department is going to need this suite. It's only fair to have it ready to move into as soon as he or she arrives."

"Then no one's been hired to replace you?" Jackson said.

"No. We're still looking at likely candidates," John replied.

The beeper on John's belt went off.

"Go ahead and answer your page," Jackson said. "I'll continue here."

Looking relieved to be free of the sorting and packing, John nodded and headed off. "Be back as soon as I can," he said over his shoulder.

"Take your time," Jackson murmured as he sat down in the midst of the memorabilia and glanced around. Truth to tell, he didn't know where to start, either.

"If I didn't know better, I'd think you were hiding out from Margaret," a familiar feminine voice drawled.

Jackson looked up to see Lacey standing in the doorway. She was wearing green scrubs and a white lab coat, a stethoscope draped around her neck. Her face was scrubbed free of makeup, and she'd caught her honey-blond hair up in a high ponytail on the back of her head. She looked very sexy in a breezy outdoorsy sort of way, even sexier than she had when she had jumped out of the cake. Jackson steeled himself against the inevitable physical reaction to her, as the ache he'd been feeling earlier resumed with throbbing intensity. He rolled to his feet, the laid-back action easing the tightness at the front of his jeans, and tucked his thumbs in the belt loops on either side of his fly. "How do you know Margaret is looking for me?" he demanded.

"Easy." Lacey ignored his narrow glance and sauntered on into the room, her running shoes silent on the carpeted floor. "She's been planning the social calendar for your vacation here for months now."

For anyone else, Jackson knew, that would have been an odd thing to decide to do, but for Margaret Ferguson-Moore, the mayor's wife and self-appointed chief meddler of Laramie, it was just par for the course. Jackson scowled. "Where does that busybody get off, acting as social director for my life?"

"My question exactly. What is the history between you two, anyway?"

Nothing I'd care to recall, Jackson thought grimly. In fact it was just this kind of tiresome childhood baggage he'd sought to avoid by practicing medicine elsewhere, because everyone knew history—especially unpleasant history—had a way of repeating itself.

"Every time I ask someone," Lacey persisted, perplexed, "they just shake their heads, roll their eyes and mutter something about Margaret still having it in for you."

"Don't you have a patient to see?" Jackson interrupted.

Lacey shook her head and announced with complacency, "I just finished rounds, and my office hours don't start for another forty minutes, so I've got all the time in the world to just hang out." She propped her hands on her slender hips. "What are you doing here, anyway?"

"I told my dad I'd help him start packing up and get ready to move out of the hospital." Jackson shrugged and looked around. "Though part of me thinks it's a futile exercise. We hadn't been in here thirty minutes when he ran off to answer a page."

Lacey studied him. "You don't want him to retire, do you?" she concluded.

Jackson pushed away a surge of conflicting feelings as he traced the engraving on the desktop nameplate bearing his dad's name.

"I just think he's awfully young."

Lacey edged closer, inundating him with the fresh scent of shampoo. "He's sixty-three."

And sharp as a tack, Jackson thought. They didn't make better diagnosticians. "He could work a few more years," Jackson muttered.

Lacey perched on the edge of John's desk and planted her hands on either side of her. "He probably will, just in another capacity. The hospital board already wants him for a spot there. And the local emergency-management group needs a new medical advisor, too. I've heard he will probably take them up on their offer to help coordinate training at the Red Cross and other volunteer groups in the area."

"Assuming, of course, he does retire, as scheduled," Jackson retorted stiffly.

Lacey turned her face up to his and studied him with a skeptical air. "You're fooling yourself if you think he doesn't really want this. Your dad has done what he set out to do here, and he's ready to move on."

"The community and the hospital need him," Jackson insisted stubbornly. And it wouldn't seem like Laramie Community Hospital without a McCabe as chief of staff.

Lacey smiled. "As a guiding force—sure. But as a physician, he's worked hard to make sure that's covered. I know when your mom and dad started the hospital years ago, they were among only a handful of employees running the place, but we've got a full nursing staff and thirteen physicians here now, including four family doctors, three emergency room physicians, a pediatrician, an obstetrician, anesthesiologist, ophthalmologist, internist and radiologist. All we need is another surgeon, to fill that opening, someone to take your dad's place, and we'll be all set. We have your mom and dad to thank for that. Their diligence, their devotion to the community, made all this possible. And now they're ready to retire—they both are."

"This hospital won't be the same without the Mc-Cabes here running things."

Lacey shrugged. "So step in and fill their shoes. Join our staff here and run for chief of staff if it pleases you. There will be an election at the end of the month, when your dad's retirement becomes official."

Jackson shook his head. He would hang out in Laramie for the next month for two reasons. One, he needed the break as well as the chance to visit with his family and friends. And two, he wanted to be there to see his parents marry all over again. But as soon as that was done, he was leaving again. "There's no way I'd trade on my mom's and dad's names and success to get a position like that."

Recognition lit Lacey's green eyes. "So that's why you won't stay." Her ponytail bobbed as she nodded her head in acknowledgment. "You don't want to compete with your dad."

Jackson scowled. There was no doubt he could trade on his parents' phenomenal legacy if he so desired. He didn't. "If I get something, it'll be on my own merit," he said shortly.

Lacey rolled her eyes. "You can prove yourself here as well as anywhere else."

Jackson was about to argue with that when he caught a glimpse of someone coming down the hall. Perdition! First that stack of invitations, now this! Swearing heatedly to himself, he swiftly stepped behind the door, out of view. As he'd half expected, the unbearably nosy Lacey Buchanon followed. Cuffing her right wrist with his left hand, he lifted his free hand to his lips commanding silence, then tugged her to stand beside him, their backs to the wall.

Lacey's blond brows drew together in confusion as she whispered impatiently, "What now?"

"Whatever you do—" being careful to remain out of sight, Jackson twisted around to face her "—don't scream."

Chapter 3

As she caught sight of the sexy promise in his sea-blue eyes, Lacey's heart pounded, and her breath stalled in her throat. *Oh, no,* she thought as she placed a staying hand upon the rock-solid wall of his chest, *not again.* "Jackson, don't—"

Jackson merely smiled, looking as if he wanted very much to forget where they were and why and haul her into his arms and kiss her again, as thoroughly and expertly as he had before. "Be a pal, Lacey," he cajoled softly, stepping closer. "Just play along, and I swear to you I'll make it worth your while."

A pal! Since when was she his pal? And what did he mean he'd "make it worth her while" Lacey wondered as Jackson sidestepped her objections and gathered her in his arms with a deft, sure touch. Already cupping the back of her head with one hand, he lifted her chin with the other. Ignoring her soft gasp of dismay, he lowered his mouth swiftly to hers.

Given they were obviously doing this for someone else's benefit, she expected his caress to be a stage kiss—full of a lot of drama and panache and very little feeling. The truth was, the embrace was anything but fake. He kissed her as if he meant it, with equal parts passion and tenderness, finesse and seduction. Despite her determination not to give in to his ruse, whoever it was for, she felt her lips part and soften beneath his, felt her body sensually mold to the length of his. And that was when the patter of footsteps came into the room, followed immediately by a heartbeat of silence, then a delicate, feminine cough.

Jackson of course, being the rogue he was, pretended not to hear. Lacey could not avoid them. Her irritation growing, Lacey gathered her wits about her and tapped him lightly and just as dramatically on the shoulder. Ever so reluctantly he lifted his head, stared down at Lacey like a fool totally besotted and falling in love.

Her heart skipped a beat.

And if she hadn't known better, she would have sworn his did, too.

Jackson smiled, turned to the very well-known woman behind them. His expression chagrined, he turned back to Lacey.

"Whoops. Looks like we just got found out, darlin'."

Lacey was not amused, either at being used or at being called darlin' for effect. Unfortunately, she knew if she didn't play along with him now, the story that Jackson had gotten the best of her by stealing a kiss or two or three or four would make the hospital, and eventually the community, grapevine. And she didn't want that, either. Bad enough she'd been kissing him on the job, so to speak.

Margaret Ferguson-Moore, the mayor's wife, and Lacey's friend since she had arrived in Laramie, continued to study them with her large gray eyes. "I didn't know the two of you knew each other at all," Margaret said, perplexed, patting the ends of her very bouffant chin-length auburn hair. If there was any Texas-style grooming tip the skinny-as-a-rail Margaret believed in, it was big hair. "Before the infamous stripper-in-the-cake incident, anyway," Margaret teased.

Lacey grinned sheepishly at the ribbing from the head of the hospital's volunteer organization, the Pink Ladies—so named because of the uniforms they now wear. "You heard about that, huh?"

"Oh, honey, puh-leese. Everyone in town knows you stripped down to practically nothing for Doc McCabe and his boys."

"It was a bikini," Jackson corrected smoothly, wreathing a proprietary arm about Lacey's shoulders. "And a very memorable gold lamé one at that!"

"I gather she did get your attention," Margaret said dryly. "If that kiss I saw just now is any indication of what went on between the two of you after Lacey lured you away from the party."

"Our kissing has nothing to do with the bikini she was wearing—although I gotta admit Lacey did look darn fine in it." He turned to Lacey and grinned, his hot glance skimming her from head to toe, before he turned back to Margaret to finish explaining. "We've been kissing," Jackson vowed, ignoring Margaret's obvious skepticism, "because Lacey and I are soul mates."

Lacey shot Jackson a look. Whatever was going on between Jackson and Margaret, he was laying it on a little thick, wasn't he? "Soul mates," Lacey repeated dryly, elbowing him in the ribs, before she turned to give him a facetiously adoring look. "Isn't it a little soon to be coming to that conclusion, honey?"

"Not too soon at all." Ignoring Lacey's sarcasm, Jackson patted Lacey's spine affectionately, then turned back to Margaret. "About that social calendar you arranged for me..." he apologized with what passed for a moue of regret. "I'm sorry. I'm going to have to let you decline all those invitations you helped set up for me. I'm going to be very busy with Lacey while I'm in Laramie, now that we've found each other. You understand."

Margaret regarded Jackson, obviously not buying his romantic ruse for one minute. "This isn't going to end it, you know," she warned him dryly, her eyes drifting momentarily to the possessive hold he had on Lacey. "I still owe you one, big-time, Jackson McCabe."

For what? Lacey wondered. She could be wrong, but it didn't look as if there had been any past romance between Jackson and Margaret. No. Whatever it was, it was something else.

"Trust me," Jackson countered to Margaret, just as meaningfully. "This should end it."

"It will end when I even the score between us, and not one single solitary second sooner," Margaret decreed flatly. Her gray eyes gleaming mischievously, she turned to Lacey and said, "You've snagged yourself quite a man."

"Oh, he's one of a kind all right," Lacey replied wryly. Even if she didn't begin to understand him!

Still grinning and shaking her head at Jackson, Margaret turned on her heel and left.

Jackson watched her go, then heaved a sigh of relief and removed his arm from her shoulders. "Thanks for playing along," he said distractedly.

"Oh, don't mention it," Lacey retorted airily as she pivoted to face him. "But if you think kissing me like there's no tomorrow comes without a price, you really are clueless."

Jackson knew their kisses had turned his world upside-down. It was something else to know they'd done the same thing for her. "That's really the way the kiss felt to you?" he asked quietly, knowing things were moving too fast, yet as powerless as she to slow them down.

"I think," Lacey explained, looking as mistrustful of fast-moving romance as he was, "that's the way you wanted me to feel."

Jackson moved closer, so they were almost touching. "And did you?" he asked, even softer.

Lacey's cheeks pinked self-consciously. For a moment she fell silent. Finally she tucked her hands in the pockets of her white lab coat and gave him a smile that divulged nothing. "What is the deal with you and Margaret?"

That, Jackson thought, was a lot harder to explain.

"What do you know about her?" he asked casually. Heading back over to the boxes he and his dad had brought in for the move, Jackson grabbed one and began filling it with books that needed to be packed.

Lacey edged closer and perched on the edge of his father's desk and, holding up a finger for each pertinent piece of data, began ticking off facts. "She's married to the mayor of Laramie and the mother of six. She's president of the Pink Ladies. There isn't an ounce of gossip around here she doesn't know. She has a warped sense of humor and a penchant for practical jokes. She's also active in every charity in Laramie and the 'go-to person' people seek out if they want to get something done around here. No one can organize or get things done like Margaret," Lacey concluded, her admiration evident.

Finished filling one box, Jackson looked around for the scissors and tape. Spying them on the desk next to Lacey, he walked over to get them. "She's also a childhood rival of mine, a real know-it-all."

Lacey moved her hip slightly, to avoid coming in contact with his arm. "Did the two of you ever date?"

"No, there was no room in the rivalry for that." Jackson went back to the box and tore off a strip of tape.

"You competed with her?" Lacey watched as he smoothed the tape across the top.

Jackson shook his head. "She competed with me, relentlessly, from kindergarten on, and she never forgave me for acing her out of the valedictorian spot, or beating her in the race for class president."

Lacey's eyes widened with pleasure. "You were both?"

He shrugged and retrieved another empty box. It was embarrassing how easily some things had come to him. "It just turned out that way."

Lacey crossed her arms in front of her. She studied him relentlessly. "That can't be all there was to it, Jackson. I know Margaret. What'd you do to her?"

Jackson did his best to suppress a mischievous smile. "What makes you think I did anything to her?" he asked innocently.

"The latent animosity," Lacey replied. "C'mon. Give, McCabe. I want the back story."

Knowing Lacey well enough by now to realize she wouldn't give up until she had her answers, Jackson reached for a sheet of the packing paper his mother had provided for the breakable objects. "I know she's sort of toned down a bit since she became a mother herself, and she is an asset to the community these days, but back when I was living here, in fact the whole time we were growing up together, she was a real pain in the butt. She was always bossing people around and telling me and everyone else what to do."

Lacey hopped down from her perch on the desk and edged closer. "I take it you didn't follow her directions."

Jackson studied the way the sunlight streaming through the windows lit up her honey-blond hair, before turning his gaze back to her face. "I did what should be done. Usually that didn't square with what she had ordered."

"And this culminated in…?" Lacey prodded curiously.

His mind more on Lacey than his task, Jackson

wrapped a framed photo and slid it into the box. "Margaret had this gossip column in the school newspaper. Usually it was about who was dating whom or who had a crush on whom. That type of thing. I thought it was totally stupid, and it really ticked me off that she kept putting my name in every week's issue, like my love life or lack thereof or whatever the case happened to be was anyone else's business!"

Lacey's soft lips curved in a slow smile. "But Margaret knew it irked you so she kept doing it."

Jackson nodded grimly. "Right. And a couple of times she really embarrassed me, as well as quite a few others. You know, trying to get people together who were never going to date in this lifetime, or publically pushing to reunite couples who had broken up when it just wasn't gonna happen." He clenched his teeth, recalling, "You know what high school's like. Everything's very dramatic. And kids' feelings—their self-esteem—gets hurt very easily. Anyway, finally I'd just had enough of her meddling and I decided to do something about it, so I got some buddies of mine to run a parody of her gossip column in the last edition of the school newspaper that year. They put a red wig and glasses on me, and made me up to sorta look like her and took my photo, which they ran with the caricature. But I wrote it under my byline."

"Only *she* was mentioned in the parodied column this time," Lacey guessed.

Jackson nodded. "Instead of being mentioned once, she was mentioned in every single item of gossip." He grinned, remembering the stir it had caused and, more important, the lesson it had taught Margaret, one he was sure was still burned into her brain to this day. "It was all pretty preposterous."

"And the other kids loved it."

"Oh, yeah." Jackson reached for another framed photo and began to wrap it, too. "Especially all those she'd previously embarrassed in print. Margaret, of course, was furious to find herself the brunt of the innuendo. She said I had completely misunderstood all she had been trying to do—which was to micromanage everyone else's love life—and she would see me at the altar before all was said and done, courtesy of her machinations, of course. Obviously that's what this is all about."

Lacey prowled the office restlessly. "She wants you to be involved with someone, and she wants to be able to take the credit."

Jackson tore his gaze from the enticing sway of her hips. "Right. So she'll have the last laugh. And the satisfaction of knowing she has prodded or 'bossed' me into the love of my life. It's also a way of getting under my skin, 'cause I've made no secret of the fact that I'm in no hurry to get married, if at all."

"Ah, the perennial bachelor," Lacey noted as silence fell between them.

Jackson nodded. Finished with another box, he straightened. "But if I were to fold…and she were in any way responsible…"

"I can see what an untenable situation that would be for you," Lacey said gravely.

"Fortunately," Jackson's lips curved with satisfaction, "you weren't on the list of people vying for my company while I'm on vacation. So by keeping company with you—and only you—while I'm in town, she has lost again. All her behind-the-scenes organizing of my social calendar has been for naught."

Lacey just looked at him and shook her head. "Has anyone ever told you to let bygones be bygones?"

Jackson scowled as his resentment of his childhood nemesis returned. "I don't care how old she is, or how long ago that was. Margaret's not going to rest until she has the last word. And I'm not letting her have it."

And they said women were ruled by their emotions, Lacey thought, rolling her eyes. "So, let me get this straight," she said in a low, deadpan voice. "You want me to pretend there is something going on between us—all this month—not to mention besmirch my reputation—"

"Hey," Jackson interrupted, looking highly insulted and thumping his chest, "being with me can only enhance your reputation."

Lacey gave him a look. "That's a subject up for debate."

"We could always try it and see," he suggested playfully.

Lacey edged closer, taking in the way his pale blue Western shirt and dark denim jeans brought out the blue of his eyes. She could tell by the way his bittersweet-chocolate-colored hair lay that it had been shampooed and brushed neatly at one point that morning—only to be rumpled around his face by either the wind or the restless combing of his fingers. His jaw was freshly shaven and scented briskly with cologne.

Lacey watched him carry one of the packed boxes

of books over to the door, the muscles of his chest and shoulders straining against the starched cotton of his shirt. "Just out of curiosity," she asked as he went to get another, "why don't you want to get married to any of the women around here? I mean, I know some of the women vying to get on the social calendar Margaret has been arranging for you, and most of them are very nice and very good-looking themselves."

"Because most of them have an agenda—whether it be to marry rich, get out of town, stay in town, or just settle down and have kids, it's still a means to an end. And I don't want to be a pawn in anyone's game."

"Very few of us do," Lacey conceded reluctantly, thinking of the way she had jumped out of that cake just to get a chance to talk to him. Pushing aside her guilt and her sudden urge to apologize—he didn't need to know she had never done anything that brazen and uninhibited in her life before—she asked him casually, "Does this mean you'll never marry?"

Jackson's glance narrowed as he picked up another box and began to fill it with photos of some of the Little League teams his dad had sponsored in recent years. "Not unless I fall head-over-heels in love with a woman and decide I can't live without her."

"And so far that hasn't happened," Lacey surmised as she picked up a sheet of packing paper and handed it to him.

A distant, brooding look crossed his ruggedly handsome features. For a long moment he was silent, then finally he said, "I've been around the block."

"And dated a lot, from what I hear."

He sent her a glance that seemed to signify resentment that she'd been probing his past, too. "But I don't keep dating a woman once I know it's not going to work out," he explained.

Lacey handed over a silver trophy from the annual Laramie Horseshoe Tournament, bearing Doc's name. "How long does it take you to figure that out?"

"Generally?" Jackson shrugged his broad shoulders. "One date. I mean at the end of it you either know it's something special or it's not."

"Ever think it was right and it wasn't?"

Jackson's eyes clouded over once again as he closed another box with tape. "I've made mistakes in the romance department." He straightened slowly and, hands on his hips, towered over her. "Who hasn't? The bottom line is I grew up here and I've known most of the women from the time they were in kindergarten. Trust me, Lacey, there is no one in Laramie for me."

"Ah." Lacey watched him carry yet another packed box to the stack next to the door. "No wonder you're headed for the big city, then."

Jackson tipped his head to the side. "I'm going to have to fall in love with someone if I want to eventually settle down," he theorized bluntly.

"And you think that's likelier in the big city," Lacey guessed, wondering why she was taking this so personally. It wasn't like she had a crush on him, after all.

"The Fort Worth-Dallas metropolitan area has almost three million people residing there. Even being as picky as I am, I ought to be able to find someone there who'll interest me, don't you think?"

Probably, Lacey thought, and found she was even more depressed about the whole situation and for reasons she didn't really want to analyze. Reasons that might have had more than a little to do with those hot, sexy kisses they had shared.

"What I think," she countered lightly, as she began to move about his father's office restlessly and tried not to think about her own past experiences in that regard, "is that big cities can be cold, cruel places."

Again, Jackson shook his head in disagreement. "Not necessarily," he said firmly.

So there they were, Lacey thought, in a mythical man-woman standoff. He was leaving soon—for good—just as he had said he would all along. And he, being the practical-minded bounder he was, still wanted to use her to foil all the eligible Laramie, Texas, women who were chasing him while he was in town.

"Look," Lacey said with exasperation, trying once again to turn the tables on him and take charge of the situation and meet her goal of finding a talented surgeon for Laramie Community Hospital, all in one fell swoop. He had promised to make that last kiss worth her while after all. "If I am going to do this—and it's still a big *if,* mind you—then you are going to have to pay me back by being on staff here temporarily and being on emergency call for the month. Or until I find a surgeon to take the job permanently. Otherwise no deal."

Jackson frowned, looking troubled again. "If I were to work here and be on staff, even temporarily, it would raise false hopes for my folks." Clearly, he didn't want to hurt them.

Lacey didn't, either, but she was desperate. With the nearest hospital some forty-five minutes away, they needed a surgeon on hand for emergencies, and they needed one now. In the end Jackson's parents would understand, and if in the meantime Jackson found practicing medicine to be more challenging at Laramie Community Hospital than he thought, so be it, Lacey thought firmly. She folded her arms in front of her. "Take it or leave it."

Jackson's stormy-blue eyes roamed her upturned face. "Have I mentioned how I hate bossy women who tend to plan out my life for me?" he asked wryly.

"Have I mentioned I don't care?" Lacey gave him a hell-for-leather smile. "Take it or leave it, bucko."

Jackson drove his fingers through his hair and released a long, heartfelt sigh. "Damn you drive a hard bargain. All right, I'll do it," he conceded finally, looking for a moment as if he'd just sold his soul. "But in return, you, my lady, are going to have to do one heck of a bang-up job driving all the other women away."

No problem, Lacey thought. She wouldn't want them to have him, anyway.

Those women—like her—deserved a man who not only loved Laramie but would stay and make it their home. Like it or not, that was definitely not Dr. Jackson McCabe.

Their bargain made, Lacey departed for her office—and the pint-size patients lining up to see her—shortly thereafter. Jackson went back to packing his father's belongings. And he was still doing so when his dad returned from being paged. Only this time he wasn't alone. This time Lilah was with him.

"What's this your mother and I hear about you and Lacey dating?" John demanded.

"Not to mention kissing! This morning! Right here in this very office!" Lilah added, looking stunned, shocked and upset all at once.

Leave it to Margaret to spread the gossip through the hospital grapevine at the speed of light, Jackson thought disparagingly. Another reason why he didn't need Margaret micromanaging his social life here in Laramie or anywhere else.

Unfortunately Jackson couldn't tell his parents the truth about what was going on between him and Lacey. They'd never go for it, not in a million years. And frankly, he wasn't all that sure it was such a good idea, either. Her kisses packed a powerful punch. One his humming body was still feeling in all the important places, and then some.

He turned away from his parents, finding it easier to honor the hard-driven bargain he'd made with Lacey Buchanon if he wasn't looking at his parents directly. "It all happened pretty fast."

"I'll say!" John retorted.

"It's nothing you need be concerned about. Lacey and I—well, we had a talk after we were sort of caught acting like a couple of kids—and we uh…we know we have to be more adult about things in the future, and we're going to be." Talk about nonanswers! Jackson thought, a little embarrassed to find himself double-speaking like an able politician.

"Your mother and I are both very fond of Lacey, and her mother, you know," John reminded his son. "We wouldn't want to see Lacey hurt by any rash behavior on your part."

And as the man in the situation, Jackson knew they were holding him fully responsible to see she wasn't. "I know, Dad," Jackson replied, pushing away the guilt he felt at ever having kissed Lacey.

Lilah's concerned look softened into a smile of pure happiness. "At any rate, I'm glad you've decided to be on call here."

His dad grinned, too. "I'm proud of you, son." John slapped him on the back. "You know it's what I've always wanted."

Jackson felt another flash of guilt. His parents were setting themselves up to be hurt, their unrealistic expectations crushed, and it was all his fault, because he couldn't keep his hands—and his kisses—to himself where the tenacious Lacey Buchanon was concerned. "It's just temporary," he cautioned his parents with a frown.

"We know, son," they said in perfect unison, looking pleased. But Jackson had serious doubts. He never wanted to hurt or disappoint his parents.

"By the way, Lacey wanted us to give you a message," John continued. "She said she passed the word to Margaret that the luncheon is okay with you, so it's all set for Thursday noon. Your mother and I will be there, too."

What luncheon? Jackson wondered, incensed. But not wanting to admit a woman had gone behind his back and done a number on him yet again, Jackson struggled to contain his temper as he inquired casually, "Lacey told you about it?"

"And we think it's an inspired idea, taking care of all your social obligations and letting Margaret do something for you in one fell swoop." His mother beamed. "This way everyone is happy, Jackson."

Except me, Jackson thought irately.

"Lacey, of course, will be there, too," John added.

Lilah smiled. "She said she wouldn't miss it for the world."

Chapter 4

Jackson was on his way back from carrying another load of boxes to the back of his dad's pickup truck when he caught sight of Lacey in the nursery several hours later. She was standing over a plexiglass bassinet, smiling and talking softly to her patient as she examined her. No doubt about it, Jackson thought as he watched Lacey gently handle the newborn baby girl. Lacey had a way with kids, and she clearly loved her work. It was hard not to respect that, he realized grudgingly, even if he did want to read her the riot act at the moment.

His heart thudding impatiently, Jackson waited until Lacey had finished checking the newborn infant's heart and lungs and removed the stethoscope from her ears before he joined her in the nursery. It pleased him to see her lips part in an O of surprise and her cheeks pinken as she reached for the baby's chart to make a few notations about what she'd found.

"You've been busy this morning," Jackson drawled, his glance leaving no doubt as to what he was referring.

The color in Lacey's cheeks deepened even more as her eyes took on a mischievous light. Putting the chart aside, she cast him a flirtatious glance. "You heard already?" Lacey quipped as she swaddled her tiny patient in a flannel blanket. As they walked away, the infant was already drifting back to sleep.

Jackson held the door for Lacey and followed her out of the nursery, into the hall. "My parents couldn't wait to tell me the delightful news."

Lacey shrugged her slender shoulders amiably, conceding, "They were happy."

Too bad I wasn't, Jackson thought irritably. He hated the thought of Margaret getting the best of him, even for a moment, and to have Lacey helping her do it, when she knew darn well how he felt about Margaret and all her machinations, made it a double whammy.

"So what is this luncheon they were talking about?" he demanded as Lacey fell in step beside him, their footsteps echoing in the quiet corridor.

Lacey's expression sobered as they turned the corridor and headed past labor and delivery rooms where Jackson's father and mother had delivered scores of infants over the years. "The Pink Ladies have recently made it tradition to give any visiting physician or new physician on staff a luncheon in his or her honor," Lacey told him matter-of-factly, turning her glance up to his. Smiling contentedly, she continued, "As soon as I told Margaret you were going to be helping out, on an emergency-call basis while you were in town vacationing, Margaret knew the Pink Ladies needed to hold a luncheon in your honor, too." Lacey paused and wrinkled her nose. "Thursday is okay, isn't it?"

It didn't matter if it was or wasn't, Jackson thought, piqued. Now that his parents knew about the fete, there was no way he could back out without embarrassing them professionally and personally, and he would do whatever he had to do to see that didn't happen. "Thursday is fine," he said tautly.

"Good—"

"Though what that has to do with my social obligations my mother indicated I'd be fulfilling at the same time, I sure as heck don't know."

"Actually, it's simple," Lacey said, as they left labor and delivery and headed for the elevators that would take them back to the doctors' office suites. Lacey punched the button. When the doors opened on an empty elevator, the two of them hopped in. As the doors slid shut, Lacey braced her hands on the rail on either side of her and turned to face him. "Since you wanted to keep the rest of your social calendar clear, I also suggested to Margaret that she invite all the women who have been wanting to get together with you to attend. Make it sort of a pot-luck affair, instead of the usual catered deal. Because I was in a generous frame of mind, you'll be happy to know I credited you with the entire idea."

Jackson was not happy about that at all, and what's more, Lacey *had* to know it. That didn't mean, however, he had to show his displeasure. "And let me guess," he said dryly, leaning against the opposite railing and telling himself it was too late to be having second thoughts about this arrangement of theirs. "Margaret went for the idea, hook, line and sinker?"

"I think she likes the idea of watching you squirm as you try to juggle a whole roomful of women lusting after you." Lacey tossed him a sexy smile, the rigid set of her spine thrusting her breasts up and out. "Actually, I think that might be kind of fun myself, which is why I've also decided to attend."

Jackson tore his eyes from the soft globes and focused on her face.

"You're forgetting one thing."

Lacey tossed her head and ignored his steady glance. "And what, pray tell, would that be?"

Jackson felt his jaw tighten. Normally he was as laid-back as they came when it pertained to his private life, but Lacey had a way of pushing his composure to the max. "As my girlfriend for the duration for my vacation here this time, you won't be just attending the luncheon, you'll be attending as my date. So if I'm squirming, pumpkin, you'll be squirming, too."

"Not necessarily." Lacey's chin lifted contentiously as the elevator stopped on their floor and the doors slid open. "For all you know, I don't have a jealous bone in my body and I like sharing my beaux."

I find that hard to believe, Jackson thought as she led the way out of the elevator. He fell into step behind her, enjoying the enticing sway of her hips for a moment, before he surged ahead to walk beside her. "Well, we'll see, won't we?" he said softly, as they turned the corner and stepped into her office.

Lacey shot him a glance over her shoulder. "I guess we will," she murmured.

Because it was during the two-hour noon break in office hours, the reception area was empty, save for Lacey's receptionist, a young man in his early twenties. "Clyde," Lacey introduced the tall, bespectacled clerk with aplomb, "this is Dr. Jackson McCabe—"

"Oh, yeah, John McCabe's son."

"Jackson, my receptionist Clyde Tynsdale."

No sooner had the two men shaken hands, than Clyde grabbed a FedEx envelope. "This is all ready to go. The letter just needs your signature." Clyde tore it from the printer, then handed it over and watched while Lacey scrawled her John Hancock at the bottom of the neatly printed page.

Lacey handed it back. "Did you get the info from the chamber of commerce?"

Clyde nodded. "As well as the public relations packet you wanted. FedEx is on their way over right now to pick it up. It'll be there by ten-thirty tomorrow morning."

"Great work, Clyde. Thank you."

Clyde beamed and pushed his glasses farther up the bridge of his nose. "No problem, Lacey."

Lacey smiled back at him. "How's the schedule looking for this afternoon?"

Clyde hit a button on his keyboard, and her appointment schedule popped up on his computer screen. "You're booked solid starting at two, so better get a lunch break while you can."

"Okay. Did those labs come back on Molly Weatherby yet?"

"On your desk."

"Thanks."

"No problem."

Lacey headed into her private office. Not the least put off, Jackson followed. She swung around to face him as she reached her desk. "You know, you can leave any time now."

"I want to know how Molly Weatherby's doing first." Was she still a possible candidate for surgery?

Lacey picked up the lab reports. She frowned as she scanned them. Molly's white count was down from last evening, but not by much.

"Problem?" Jackson guessed.

Lacey handed the papers over with a sigh. "Actually, yes. I know you're trying to keep one foot out the door here, but how would you feel about giving a second opinion?" This was one time when she could definitely use a surgeon's expertise.

"Hi, darlin'." Lacey greeted her five-year-old patient softly from the doorway of her hospital room.

Molly Weatherby looked up from the book her mother had been reading to her. If possible, her skin was even more chalky and washed-out than it had been the previous evening. There were shadows beneath her eyes and a sad, dejected expression on her young face. "Hi, Dr. Lacey," Molly said listlessly.

Concerned—Lacey had hoped to see more improvement in her young patient by now—Lacey strode into the room, Jackson McCabe right behind her. "Remember Dr. Jackson from last night?" Lacey asked Molly cheerfully.

Molly nodded and tightened her little fingers until they pinched the edge of her book. "Uh-huh." Molly tucked Teddy Beddy closer to her chin and regarded Jackson warily.

"Well, he came by to look in on you this morning, too. Okay?"

Molly nodded. "Hi, Dr. Jackson."

Jackson smiled at the girl. "Hi, Molly." He nodded at Patricia Weatherby. "Hi, Molly's mom."

Patricia smiled and continued holding her daughter's head and shoulders cradled in the curve of her arms. "Hello, Dr. Jackson."

Motioning for Molly and her mom to stay just as they were, Lacey sat down on the edge of the hospital bed, put her stethoscope in her ears. Lacey moved Molly's hospital gown aside and listened to her tummy. Finished, she removed the stethoscope from her ears and laced it around her neck. "How's your belly feeling now? Is it still hurting?"

"No." Molly sighed, even more listlessly. "It feels fine."

Lacey did a quick physical exam and found that to be true—there was no rebound tenderness today. And yet… "You didn't eat any breakfast this morning." Lacey glanced at Molly's lunch tray, which had been pushed to one side of the room and was awaiting pickup. "Lunch, either."

Molly's lower lip pushed out truculently. "That's 'cause I can't. Every time I try, I feel icky, like I'm gonna throw up again."

"We can give you something for that," Lacey said gently. "I'll have the nurse add some phenergan to your

IV and that should make the icky feeling go away." Lacey smiled encouragingly. "Maybe then you'll be able to eat some broth or some Jell-O."

"Yuck! I hate broth and the Jell-O is green."

Lacey grinned. It looked like their patient was getting grumpy. That was always a good sign. "I can see where that would be a problem," she said dryly, making a final notation about her findings on Molly's chart and handing it over to Jackson to peruse. "What color do you like?"

Molly's gaze turned even crankier as she rubbed her eyes. "Only orange. No other color!"

Lacey and Jackson both grinned at the adamant response. No one could say little miss Molly didn't know her own mind or tastes. "Okay, now that we've got that covered, sweetie, what would you like to drink?" Lacey persisted, knowing they had to get Molly taking—and tolerating—fluids by mouth before they could remove the IV. Given her frame of mind, it didn't look like that was going to be an easy task, since her usual beverages of choice—fruit juice and milk—were clearly outlawed for the moment. "Do you like Seven-Up?"

"I only like cherry Seven-Up," Molly replied, abruptly looking like she was going to cry. "And they don't have that here, they already said."

That, Lacey thought, was something they could do something about. "Not to worry, honey," Lacey promised firmly, patting her tiny hand. "We'll get you some." Even if she had to have it delivered herself. "In fact, I'll take care of it right now."

"Meantime, mind if I take a look at your tummy, too?" Jackson asked Molly.

Molly looked at Lacey and Lacey nodded, signaling it was a very good idea to have Jackson's input on her case.

"Okay," Molly said, but she still looked like she was going to cry.

With a look that indicated he was every bit as mindful of Molly's precarious emotional state as Lacey was, Jackson handed Molly's chart back to Lacey, then borrowed Lacey's stethoscope. With Molly still looking like she wanted to burst into tears at any second, he took a listen, then palpated Molly's abdomen with the same gentle efficiency Lacey had employed. There, Lacey soon discovered, the similarities in their two exams ended.

"Hmm," Jackson mused thoughtfully at length. He looked back at Molly's tummy and frowned like he had just uncovered something truly astounding.

Lacey saw the mischief playing around the edges of his sensual lips and wondered what he was up to now.

"What?" little Molly demanded curiously at once, forgetting for the first time since they had been in there just how pitiful she was feeling at the moment.

"I think you have an inny," Jackson announced incredulously as he pointed to Molly's belly button. He turned and regarded Lacey with mounting—but playful—urgency. "Dr. Lacey, make a note of that on the chart. This young lady has an inny, not an outy."

Lacey chuckled as she wrote it down.

Molly peered at Jackson. "What kind of belly button do you have?" Molly demanded.

"An outy," Jackson said. He turned and looked at Lacey. "And you?"

Lacey looked at him with an I-know-that-you-know glare.

Jackson looked at Mrs. Weatherby for her input. "Inny," she said

"Innies win," Jackson said.

Molly frowned. "Is my belly button making me sick?"

Jackson laughed. "Nope. Some bad old germs are making you sick, but we're getting rid of them. I was just being silly there for a minute." He tweaked the end of her nose. "I just wanted to see if I could make you smile, and I did, didn't I?"

Molly grinned. "Will you come back with Dr. Lacey and see me again?"

"Sure will. Meantime, I'm going to help Dr. Lacey get you some more medicine for your IV. And then we're going to find you some orange Jell-O and cherry Seven-Up, okay?"

Accepting the thanks of Mrs. Weatherby, Jackson and Lacey stepped out into the hall. "What do you think?"

"Same as you. I think it's most likely acute viral gastroenteritis. And if it is, she'll probably continue to get better."

Patricia Weatherby stepped out into the hall to join them. Lacey briefed her on the latest lab results, including the fact that both Molly's white count and temperature, while still elevated, were down slightly from the day before.

Patricia's shoulders sagged in relief. "When do you think Molly'll be okay again?" she asked.

Jackson and Lacey exchanged a glance. "It's hard to

say exactly," Lacey replied. "Viruses like this usually just have to run their course, but we're hoping to see a lot of improvement in the next twenty-four hours."

"Enough for her to be released from the hospital?" Patricia asked anxiously. Hands cupped beneath opposite elbows, she paced back and forth.

"Maybe," Lacey said. At least she hoped so. "But before that happens," she cautioned, "Molly will have to be looking and feeling a lot better. She'll have to be able to take fluids by mouth and keep them down. And we'd like to see her temperature back down to normal as well."

Patricia sighed and looked a lot more upset.

"I know you don't have insurance—" Lacey guessed at the root of the problem.

"It's a lot more than that." Patricia paused and bit her lip. "You know I was en route to a new job in California when Molly got sick."

Lacey nodded, remembering Patricia telling her as much the day before. "Right."

"Well, I'm supposed to be there day after tomorrow. And we've still got over twenty four hours left of driving to do."

Lacey held up a cautioning hand. "Look, even if Molly improves one hundred percent by tomorrow, there's no way you can safely put her back in the car for such a long drive immediately after dismissal."

Patricia looked even more troubled. "That's what I was afraid of," she said softly, her concern for her daughter evident.

"Look, I'm sure if you call your employer and ex-

plain the situation, they'll understand," Lacey continued sympathetically.

"I hope so." Patricia Weatherby hurried off.

Lacey turned back to Jackson. She was still holding Molly's chart, with the new orders written on it,
and for a moment their glances meshed. "Got plans for
lunch?" he asked quietly.

Her pulse picking up at the possibility-filled tone of
his voice, Lacey nodded and glanced at her watch. "I'm
meeting a friend," she said truthfully. *One you probably wouldn't want to be around. And I'm already late.*

Jackson continued to regard her with a steady, analyzing look—one that told her he knew why she was
avoiding spending time with him on a personal level
whenever possible, and why. Because the truth was she
didn't want to think about the kisses they had already
shared, and the truth was that whenever she was with
him like this, thinking about those kisses and the potential for others was all she did.

"Some other time then," he told her with infuriating
confidence.

Lacey caught a whiff of his cologne as she stepped
around him. The crisp, bracing scent was as invigorating as his touch. And just as compelling. Flushing
self-consciously, she pushed aside her attraction and
turned away. "Some other time."

"Don't say it," Lacey told Margaret when she ran
into her in the hospital cafeteria a few minutes later.

"Now, Lacey, you know me. Well-meaning busybody that I am, I can't resist commenting about and
worrying over everything that goes on around here.

Besides," Margaret put her tray down on the table and took a chair opposite Lacey, "it's no surprise Jackson McCabe set his sights on you the moment he hit town. He's always been extremely competitive in every aspect of his life."

Lacey knew she was a challenge to the opposite sex, as she'd never intended to give her heart and soul to anybody but the most deserving man, whom, unfortunately, she had yet to even come close to finding. "Funny," Lacey quipped in a low deadpan voice, "he says the same thing about you."

Margaret shrugged and smiled. "See? Then I would know, since it takes one to know one. And if you want my honest opinion, it makes sense that, being the ultracompetitive guy that Jackson is, he would go for the one single woman in town who wasn't already lusting after him."

Lacey hadn't wanted to even meet the infamous Jackson McCabe, never mind pretend to date him for the month! In fact, if he hadn't been the surgeon the community so desperately needed and wanted on the hospital staff, she wouldn't have given two cents for the news he was coming back to town; certainly would never have lined up to meet him, along with every other woman in town. And if he had agreed to talk with her about the surgeon's position on the phone or in person, she never would have jumped out of that cake to get his attention or lassoed him to a chair. But he'd forced her hand and she had gotten his attention— boy, had she gotten his attention!—and now they were going to have to deal with that.

"So you're saying I present a challenge to Dr. Jackson McCabe," Lacey paraphrased dryly as she added extra lemon to her iced tea.

Margaret dug into her salad with gusto, enjoying the meal as much as Lacey's discomfiture. "Don't play coy with me, Lacey Buchanon. You know you do."

Lacey sighed wearily, acknowledging to herself this was so. The truth was she didn't want to get involved with a star like Jackson, who was always going to be number one in his own orbit. And heaven knew, surgeons were particularly egocentric. They had to have total confidence in themselves in order to be able to do the kind of work they did. Unfortunately most surgeons she knew weren't just confident to the point of being overbearing in an operating room; they brought the same superconfidence to every aspect of their life, and that could be very maddening indeed.

"I guess I do present a challenge where Jackson is concerned," Lacey admitted reluctantly, as she picked up her grilled-chicken sandwich. "But you, friend, have an agenda here, too."

Margaret grinned sheepishly, quickly swallowing a mouthful of salad. "Okay, it's true. I was paying Jackson back for the ultimate prank he played on me, back in high school. There's a part of me that can't bear him having the last word or laugh even now. But I was also acting on behalf of Jackson and his folks in trying to organize his social invitations and hence his ability to spend time with all the available women in town. I don't think Jackson has realized it yet, but he'll never be happy anywhere else. He belongs here. Laramie is the kind of place where Jackson can really make a difference, and Jackson is the kind of guy who needs to make a difference."

Lacey could see that about Jackson, too. She admired not only his reputation as a crackerjack young surgeon, but also the compassionate way he'd dealt with Molly Weatherby. But Laramie wasn't the only place in Texas to practice medicine. And they needed to face that—she already had.

"He can do the same good in Fort Worth, too," Lacey pointed out sagely. Which was why she had already taken the additional steps to fill the surgeon's slot at Laramie Community Hospital, pronto.

"But there are tons of surgeons in Fort Worth," Margaret protested. Finished with her salad, she pushed it aside. "Here, he'd be it." Margaret rolled her eyes. "Talk about being able to save the day! If Jackson got a taste of that kind of hero worship, there's no way he'd be able to resist it."

Lacey could see Jackson lapping it up. He'd probably like it as much as he had enjoyed their passionate kisses.

"Talking about me again, huh, ladies?"

Margaret grinned at the interruption. "Hello, Jackson." She glanced at her watch and stood. Apparently unable to resist, she added with feigned enthusiasm, "Imagine the two of us squaring off in the cafeteria again, every day at noon." She patted him on the shoulder. "It's just like old times, isn't it?"

At the sarcastic note in Margaret's voice, it was all Lacey could do to stifle a groan. Giving him no chance to reply, Margaret picked up her tray. "See you later, girlfriend." She winked at Lacey and moved off.

"Another reason why I could never live here again," Jackson muttered beneath his breath as he set his own tray down and pulled up a chair opposite Lacey. "I had enough of some people back in high school."

Lacey tried not to think about how pleased she was to see him again. "Childhood animosities are no reason to do—or not do—anything," Lacey reprimanded coolly.

Jackson arched a dissenting brow as he dug into his chili and corn bread. "You didn't spend thirteen years in a class with Margaret."

"No," Lacey countered, still studying Jackson pointedly. In the sunny cafeteria his eyes seemed an even lighter shade of sea-blue. "But I eat lunch with Margaret here almost every day and enjoy her company, and I see what a valuable asset she is to this community. If you were adult enough to let bygones be just that, you might enjoy her camaraderie, too."

Jackson shook his head, nixing her suggestion of a truce before he'd even had time to really absorb it. "I wouldn't count on it," he countered dryly, shaking red pepper flakes and Tabasco sauce onto his bowl of chili. "Besides, I'm ready for new vistas," he told her, meeting her slightly disapproving look with one of his own. "And I notice you didn't go back to wherever it was you grew up," he countered archly.

Lacey pushed the unhappy memories away and drew a tremulous breath. "I grew up in the Dallas area. And you're right. I don't want to go back there. I much prefer life in a small, Texas town."

"You say that now," Jackson predicted, his eyes on hers. "Wait till you've been here a while and everyone in town knows everything about you and your private life. Then you might be singing a different tune."

Lacey had to admit there were things about her past, particularly her post-med-school life in Dallas, that she didn't want revealed to the people here in Laramie. But there was no use thinking about any of that now.

She turned her glance away and couldn't help but notice the woman taking a seat at a table in the far corner, a tissue clenched tightly in her hand. "Hey, isn't that Patricia Weatherby?" Lacey frowned, then turned back to Jackson. "Is it my imagination? Or does she look like she's been crying?"

"Is everything okay?" Jackson asked Patricia as he and Lacey approached.

"Is Molly okay?" Lacey persisted, aware if there was a problem of any sort she hadn't been paged.

Patricia nodded as she dabbed at the new flood of tears sliding down her cheeks. "Molly's fine. The medicine they put in her IV took away her nausea. She had a little cherry Seven-Up and orange gelatin then fell fast asleep. The nurse suggested I step out for a minute and get some lunch—" Patricia's voice caught. Abruptly she looked down at the nearly untouched sandwich on her tray and started crying again.

"Hey now," Jackson soothed as he and Lacey pulled up chairs on either side of Patricia. He patted her shoulder gently. "I know the food in the cafeteria isn't all that great," he teased, "but it's nothing to cry over."

Patricia laughed weakly and blew her nose. "The food here is fine. It's my job that's the problem. The TV station where I was going to work has rescinded its offer. They said if I couldn't get there and start work immediately, as previously scheduled, then I could just forget it. And now I don't know how I'm going to pay the hospital bill."

Lacey knew full well how it felt to be worried about money every second of every day. "Do you think it would help if we called the TV station manager for you and explained what's going on with your little girl?" she asked gently.

"I already tried that. They don't care. They're only concerned about their falling ratings, and now I don't know what I'm going to do." Patricia shook her head in regret and continued in a low, tortured voice. "I've been such a fool. If I hadn't been so in love with Cal— Molly's daddy—I wouldn't be in this mess!"

"Can't he help?" Lacey asked.

Patricia shook her head. "Cal's the reason we're in this predicament. I gave up my job as a television news producer to be with him. He wanted me to travel with him. He said he was going to divorce his wife and marry me."

"But he didn't," Lacey guessed, knowing what it was like to be promised marriage by someone who did not follow through on it.

"No. She wouldn't give him a divorce. And by then I was pregnant with Molly and it all got so complicated." She shook her head, recalling. "I knew Cal loved me, loved Molly. He'd bought us this beautiful little house in Houston. And he was with us whenever he was in town—his family lived in Louisiana. He was so good to Molly and good to me I convinced myself it didn't matter if we ever married. After all, I had the 'family'

I'd always wanted. And Cal told me——he promised me——that Molly and I would always be taken care of, no matter what, he had seen to it and put us in his will."

"But that isn't what happened?"

Patricia's hand shook as she sipped her glass of iced tea. "It turned out he never got around to making those changes to his will, at least not in any legal manner, and when he died suddenly last year, in a plane crash, and his wife found out about us, well…everything changed overnight. All my bank accounts were closed, Molly and I were evicted from the house we were living in. They even took my car and furniture away. I sold what little jewelry he'd given me——thank heavens they didn't know about that!——and finally found another job as a television news producer, and we were headed out to California to make a new life for ourselves. And now this." She began crying again. "Well, it's a disaster. Just an absolute disaster!"

"Maybe you could find a job with another TV station——"

Again, Patricia shook her head, nixing the likelihood of that. "I was in the business for such a short time. I had so little actual work experience. And it's such a competitive field! It took me months of effort, and every bit of cash reserve I had left, to find this."

"Do you have family or friends you could call?"

"No, no family. That's why Cal was so important to me. As for our friends——" Patricia's lip curled bitterly "——they began deserting Molly and me as soon as our financial circumstances changed. Guess they weren't really friends after all."

Lacey felt Jackson's eyes on hers and realized she

was revealing too much of her own haunted past by the brooding look she hadn't thought to check. Damn.

Ignoring the heated nature of his gaze, she leaned toward Patricia urgently and did what she wished someone had done for her and her mother once upon a time. "Look, there's no reason for you and Molly to panic just yet. Laramie isn't the kind of town that throws good people out. Jackson and I—we'll help you figure something out."

"Yes," Jackson added firmly, "we will."

Jackson and Lacey exchanged committed glances, glad they were in agreement on this.

"In the meantime," Lacey continued gently, "you can stay with my mother when Molly is released from the hospital. She has an apartment over the bakery on Main Street."

Patricia looked stunned and grateful all at once. "We couldn't impose."

Lacey understood that feeling, too. "Then work out some sort of barter arrangement with my mom while you're there," she suggested practically, knowing her mother well enough to know that would be fine, too. "My mom can always use a little help in her bakeshop. Staying in Laramie a little while longer will give you and Molly time to recoup, work out a payment plan with the hospital and find another job. And it'll give my mother a chance to be around a little girl again. You wouldn't believe how much she wants a grandchild to fuss over. And since she doesn't have any yet, you'd be doing me a big favor on that score." Lacey grinned enthusiastically. "So what do you say?"

Patricia paused and bit her lip. Clearly, she wanted

to jump at the offer. "You're sure it'd be all right?" she pressed. "You don't have to call and ask your mother first?"

Lacey thought about Isabel's unlimited stores of both energy and compassion. "Are you kidding? She lives for this stuff!"

Chapter 5

The next time Lacey saw Jackson it was five-thirty and he was dressed in green surgical scrubs. "So what have you been up to?" Lacey asked, trying hard to ignore his swaggering, all-male posture and loose-limbed stride.

Jackson stopped just short of her and grinned down at her insolently. "They needed some help in the emergency room. Rafe Marshall—you probably know him—he's the principal over at the elementary school—lacerated his leg pretty badly in a mishap with a chain saw. He fell off a ladder while trying to trim a tree branch that was hitting his roof. Anyway, it was not a pretty sight and more than the E.R. docs could handle alone, so I pitched in, took him up to the O.R. and helped repair the damage."

Lacey did indeed know Rafe. There wasn't a nicer educator—or single dad—in all of Laramie. His eight-year-old twins were patients of hers. "Is he going to be okay?" she asked, concerned.

Jackson nodded as if there'd never been any doubt. "Good as new," he reported happily. "Ray weathered the surgery just fine. They just moved him out of recovery and into a private room. Neighbors are taking care of the kids."

Lacey turned her head away, trying not to notice how well the cotton V-neck shirt clung to the sculpted muscles of Jackson's shoulders and chest. To no avail. Even when she wasn't looking at him, she couldn't erase the way the loose drawstring pants draped his flat stomach and the taut muscles of his long, lean legs. Jackson McCabe was sexy as could be, and now that he'd gone the extra mile and operated on Rafe, he'd be a local hero as well.

Unbidden, Lacey recalled Margaret's words. *Laramie is the kind of place where Jackson can really make a difference... Jackson is the kind of guy who needs to make a difference...*

"Sounds like you really saved the day," Lacey said lightly, wondering all the while if it really was possible…would Jackson change his mind and decide to forgo the lure of the big city and, realizing how much he was needed here, stay in Laramie after all? The expression on his face gave no clue.

"And now that I have lived up to my part of our bargain, at least for today, it's time you lived up to yours, darlin'."

Lacey's spine stiffened. She did not like the sound of that. Ignoring the sudden racing of her heart, she continued on down the hall. "I don't know what you mean."

Jackson quickly caught up and fell into step beside her, adjusting his longer strides to hers. "Do the math."

"I beg your pardon?" Lacey said tartly. Lacey had agreed to this little "arrangement" of Jackson's in order to provide the hospital with a surgeon, but she had never dreamed he'd be so hard to handle.

"I'm only going to be in Laramie for a month." As the two of them neared the staff locker room, Jackson shoved open the door, grabbed her wrist and tugged her inside. The door shut with a soft whoosh behind them, leaving them—for the moment, anyway—very much alone. Sliding his fingers from her wrist to her hand, he looked down at her and said, "Therefore, if I'm as interested in you as we want everyone to believe, I'm going to want to see you every evening and then some."

Doing that would make it seem like they were really dating. And that would lead to more kisses. Lacey could not risk more kisses. "That's sweet." Lacey withdrew her hand from his and patted Jackson's face. "But I'm busy tonight."

"With me."

"No." Lacey enunciated the word slowly. "At home."

"You're refusing to have dinner with me?"

Lacey had been to hell and back once before, when she got romantically involved with the most popular guy around. She wasn't doing it again, especially when she knew she would only be deserted in the end—again. "Looks like," she replied breezily, keeping her emotions tightly in check.

"Too bad. I was beginning to like helping out here."

Jackson took off his V-necked shirt, then—hands on the waist of his green surgical trousers—started to take those off, too.

Lacey grabbed Jackson's hands to stop him, but not before her hands brushed the smooth warm skin of his waist and abs. Having successfully stopped the shucking of his pants in front of her, she stepped back and swallowed around the sudden dryness in her throat. Her eyes lasered in on his. "You'd really walk out on this hospital if I renege?"

Jackson looked down at her. "If you break your promise to me? In a heartbeat."

Lacey blew out a disgruntled breath and moved to the other side of the long wooden bench between the rows of metal lockers. The fairness of his attitude was something she prefered not to dwell on, considering what he was threatening to do—walk out on them in their time of need.

"You are so self-absorbed!" she fumed, balling her hands into fists.

Jackson tossed his shirt into the laundry hamper. "That, my darlin' Lacey, is a subject up for discussion, but meantime, I believe in being compensated for my time and trouble and so should you."

Ignoring the sight of his lightly tanned chest, Lacey glanced at her watch. "Even so, I'm serious about having things to do tonight."

Jackson leaned closer and said with a leering grin, "Working out of the old cake again, huh?"

Unbidden, memories of the previous night flashed in Lacey's mind, and along with them, the exhilarating excitement she'd felt as she popped out of the cake, and spied Jackson McCabe standing at the bar. He'd looked faintly bored and restless until his gaze had skimmed the length of her. Then his head had lifted, his glance had ever so slowly roved her face, and his eyes had met hers. The music pounding in her ears had been nothing compared to the pounding of her heart as their gazes had locked and held. But she couldn't think about that now, Lacey schooled herself firmly, any more than she could think about the sexy mat of dark hair that feathered his muscled chest and arrowed sexily down to disappear into the low-slung waistband of his pants.

"So, who are you tying up tonight?" Jackson teased, his low voice as captivating as his smile.

"Not you." Lacey enunciated each word crisply.

"Shucks." Jackson gave her a wicked smile, as if he couldn't resist teasing her again. He snapped his fingers in mock disappointment. "And here I was, all primed for a little excitement."

Lacey gave him a quelling look. She didn't care how sexy he was! She was not going to let him seduce her or turn her into a quivering mass of vulnerability. "As a matter of fact," she countered stiffly, beginning to pace the small area restlessly, "I have things to do at home."

Jackson shrugged and fell in step beside her. "Then I'll go with you. Seeing as we're so smitten with each other, we can't bear to be apart."

Lacey rolled her eyes. If he had noticed the chill in her attitude, he was ignoring it. "You wish."

"Then, after you do whatever it is you have to do," he continued affably, refusing to take no for an answer as he reached into the locker and pulled out the pale blue western shirt he'd been wearing earlier, "we'll go somewhere together and have dinner."

Lacey could see he wasn't going to give up. And he was right, they had made a deal. He'd lived up to his end of it by pitching in and operating on Rafe Marshall. Now it was her turn to make good.

"Fine," she agreed, telling herself she could handle a simple dinner with him. "Whatever. But it'll have to be later."

Jackson looked at her as if this were definitely a problem. "How late?" he asked flatly.

"I don't know." Refusing to let Jackson—or the hopelessly romantic farce they'd bartered themselves into get to her—Lacey shrugged. She figured out all she had left to do before leaving the hospital for the day and then said reluctantly, "Seven maybe."

Dark brow furrowing, Jackson glanced at his watch. "If that's the case, then I'm going to have to make a phone call."

To whom, Lacey wondered, struggling to contain her curiosity about what else he had planned. But he made no move to enlighten her. And they parted company, the mystery intact.

"Uh-huh." Jackson laid down the law the moment they stepped outside. "No bicycling tonight. I'm squiring you around in my car."

"More opportunity to be seen?" Lacey quipped, unable to help but notice how handsome Jackson looked in the wash of summer sunlight. During the time they'd been apart, he had finished changing back into the clothes he'd had on earlier in the day—a pale blue Western shirt, dark denim jeans, handcrafted leather boots. He'd also tugged a stone-colored Stetson low on his brow, which, when combined with the unending mischief sparkling in his sea-blue eyes and the five o'clock shadow now lining his jaw, only added to his rakish aura.

"It's a pretty evening. Perfect for riding around with the top down."

Finding the brisk, spicy scent of his aftershave a little too distracting, Lacey backed up a step. "We'd get plenty of fresh air if you bicycled, too."

"True," Jackson allowed readily enough, stroking his jaw, "but I don't have a bike. All I have is a horse, and that's back at my parents' ranch. 'Course, I could ride on your handlebars or vice versa, but that could get a little tricky."

Lacey could just see herself falling bottom first into his lap or vice versa. No, they didn't want that to happen. There was enough friction of the delicious variety between them already. She planted both her hands on her hips and angled her chin up at him feistily. "You're just bound and determined to make my life harder, aren't you?" In fact, he was disrupting it in every way he could.

"Easier, Lacey," Jackson corrected as he towered over her and leaned closer still. "In every way."

Tingles of excitement raced over Lacey's skin as she imagined Jackson actually appointing himself her protector. "If that's the case, you should let me off the hook with this dating business," she said sagely, digging in her heels as he took her hand in his.

"Not a chance, lady." Jackson opened the door on

the passenger side of his low slung black Porsche. His blue eyes darkened with a fiercely possessive light. "I like the idea of you being my woman."

His woman. Lacey's throat went dry. "About that—" she began in a strangled tone as she slid into the passenger seat.

Jackson shut her door, then circled around to climb behind the wheel. "Yes?"

Lacey swallowed as he fit his car key in the ignition. "My mom is sort of old-fashioned. She doesn't believe in having red-hot love affairs."

Jackson started the car. "You've discussed this with her?" he asked in surprise.

"No," Lacey replied, as the fresh June air swept over them, "but I know how she thinks, Jackson. And my mom is marriage-minded all the way. So—"

Jackson held up a hand, palm out. "Not to worry, Lacey. I'll be a perfect gentleman around your mom, and mine, too."

Lacey breathed a sigh of relief and relaxed in the deep leather seat. "Thanks."

Jackson guided the Porsche out of the space and drove out of the parking lot. "We don't want to give the gossips too much to talk about."

"No," Lacey agreed firmly. "We don't." Even though she could, in a completely hypothetical way of course, imagine herself being involved in a red-hot love affair with him ASAP. Fortunately, imagining something— in theory—did not make it so. Did not nearly make it so, Lacey reassured herself firmly. Because this was just not a possibility for her, no matter how sexy and attractive a man Jackson was, no matter how delicious his kisses, or tender and seductive his embrace. He was leaving Laramie. She was staying. After this month they'd probably never see each other, or at least not very often. If and when she got involved with someone again it was going to be for keeps. Forever. And Jackson McCabe was most definitely not offering her that!

"This it?" Jackson guided his car into the space by the white brick building with the sparkling picture windows and the green-and-white awning. A sign above the shop bore a Texas bluebonnet and the words Isabel's Bakeshop.

Jackson cut the engine and nodded at the petite woman hanging the Closed sign on the door. She was in faded denim overalls, sneakers and a pastel T-shirt with the shop logo across the front. "That your mom?"

Lacey nodded. "Yes." At fifty-three, Isabel Buchanon's honey-blond curls were threaded liberally with silver streaks, and the smile lines around her eyes were a little deeper, but she showed no signs of slowing down. And in fact had only seemed to find more energy since she entered her fifties.

Jackson waved and came around to get Lacey's door. Together they walked up the sidewalk to greet Isabel. "Mom, I'd like you to meet Jackson McCabe."

"How do you do, Jackson?" Isabel graciously extended her hand.

"Jackson—my mom, Isabel," Lacey continued.

"A pleasure to meet you, Mrs. Buchanon." Jackson shook Isabel's hand warmly.

"Likewise." Isabel beamed. She ushered them inside, her sneaker-clad feet padding softly across the gleaming wood floor of the shop. "I've heard a lot about you, Jackson. Your parents talk about you all the time. They're very proud of you."

"And I of them."

Isabel stepped behind the long glass-fronted counters. "Can I interest you in a freshly baked cookie, Jackson?"

He studied the enticing selection still on display. "Don't mind if I do."

"So, the two of you are an item." Isabel brought out the fudge pecan and oatmeal butterscotch cookies they'd selected.

Lacey paused, her cookie halfway to her mouth. "How'd you hear that?"

"Margaret stopped in," Isabel replied as she headed for the backroom where all the baking was done.

Jackson gave Lacey a look, then leaned sideways until his shoulder brushed hers in a slow, sensual manner. "What did I tell you?" he said under his breath. "She's a busybody."

"But I also heard it from John and Lilah McCabe," Isabel continued from the other room as she went around shutting off lights. "They stopped in to pick up a cake on the way home."

"Another thing I hate about small towns," Jackson whispered in Lacey's ear. "No privacy."

"How about another cookie, Jackson?" Isabel asked sweetly. She came back with two tall glasses. "A macadamia nut white chocolate chip this time?"

Jackson grinned, all too ready to be talked into that. "Don't mind if I do."

"And some milk to wash it down?"

Jackson nodded. "That'd be perfect, thanks."

Lacey frowned. "Don't spoil him, Mom. He'll just come back."

Isabel's eyes sparkled as she filled the glasses with icy cold milk and handed them over. "Honey, if the two of you are as attracted to each other as I think you are, that's the idea."

Jackson grinned and looked at Lacey. "I like this woman," he drawled.

Isabel beamed.

Upstairs, the family quarters were small but cozy. Photos of Lacey and her mom were everywhere. Some of the older ones, taken when Lacey was a child, even had a man in them, Jackson noted.

Jackson studied the handsome, golden-haired man. He was holding a tennis racquet in one photo, two-year-old Lacey dancing around his knees. The second sported the three of them sitting in the back of a pleasure boat. The third showed him emerging from an airport jetway, wearing a suit and tie. A garment bag looped over his shoulder, he was carrying a briefcase in one hand, a large teddy bear in the other. A five-year-old Lacey and a much younger Isabel were running to greet him. Clearly, both Lacey and her mom had loved him very much. "Is this your dad?" Jackson asked.

Lacey nodded, sorrow briefly tingeing her eyes. "He died when I was eight."

"I'm sorry. That must have been hard," Jackson said softly, seeing the sudden strain on both women's faces.

Taking a deep breath, Lacey nodded, admitting this was so. She turned away, the subject closed, and followed her mother over to the floral sofa. "Mom, I did something without your permission."

Isabel paused in the act of sitting down. "Who did you offer to help out this time?"

"Patricia Weatherby and her little girl, Molly." Lacey settled opposite her mom. Briefly she explained how Patricia Weatherby had lost her job, and how upset she'd been.

"Poor woman," Isabel murmured with heartfelt sympathy when Lacey had finished filling her in. "Down to her last dime, then her daughter gets sick and has to be hospitalized and she loses her job mid-move."

"I know," Lacey concurred sadly, shaking her head.

Jackson noted both Lacey and her mom really seemed to know what the Weatherbys were feeling. Were they just naturally compassionate, or was it something more, he wondered curiously.

"But where will they sleep?" Isabel said, frowning.

"My room." Lacey hopped up cheerfully from her perch. "Which means of course I'm going to have to clear my things out."

"Where will you sleep?" Isabel stood, too.

"In one of the on-call rooms at the hospital." Lacey held up a hand. "And you can't let them know I'm doing that, either. If they thought they were putting me out of a room, they'd never accept." Motioning for both Jackson and Isabel to follow, Lacey led the way down a short hallway off the living room, past the pink-and-white bathroom, to one of the two bedrooms at the rear of the apartment. "Anyway, it'll be just for a few days," Lacey assured breezily, "till Molly is completely recovered and Patricia finds another job or figures out what she is going to do. Meantime," Lacey said as she got down on her hands and knees. She lifted the dust ruffle on the double bed, rummaged around, sneezed twice, then emerged victorious with a slightly dusty brown leather suitcase that had seen better days. "We're going to make this look like a guest room."

Jackson forced his eyes from her heart-shaped fanny and moved so he wouldn't have such an enticing view. "You're moving everything you have out?"

Lacey dusted herself and got to her feet. Hands on her hips, she glanced around the austerely furnished room. "It won't take long."

Isabel rolled her eyes. "That's an understatement if I ever heard one."

Lacey looked at Jackson and explained, "I like to live simply."

Isabel's disapproving frown deepened. "Like a nun who's taken vows of poverty is more like it."

Lacey ignored her mother's remark and said to Jackson, "Make yourself useful and give me a hand here, will you?"

She marched past a neatly made-up double bed, piled with homemade quilts, then threw open a closet and pulled out a pair of navy flats. Going to the bureau, she took out two pairs of jeans and two white V-neck T-shirts, socks and a larger stack of no-frill cotton undies.

"And grab my dress, will you? I'm going to need it for the luncheon."

Jackson headed for the closet. "Which dress?"

Isabel smiled ruefully. "These days there's only the one, if you don't count the short white leather number she borrowed from a friend for last night." Hands tucked in the front pockets of her denim overalls, Isabel lounged in the doorway. "And it's a running argument between us."

A blush sweeping into her cheeks, Lacey swiveled around, hands on her hips. "Mom, you do not have to tell him everything just because I have a date with him tonight."

Jackson grinned and opened the closet door. "I don't mind."

Isabel pointed to the navy blue dress, hanging beside a khaki skirt, two pairs of walking shorts, and a cotton madras jumper. Long sleeved, knee-length, the cotton gabardine dress was tailored in a way that never went out of style. "That dress has gotten more wear than the tires on my car."

The blush staining Lacey's cheeks got even pinker. "It's a great dress, Mom, perfect for any and all occasions."

Jackson thought it was also serviceable and plain.

Isabel turned curious eyes to his. "What do you think, Jackson?"

Jackson shrugged, knowing it wasn't his place to tell Lacey how to dress even if he did think she was shortchanging herself terribly. "I think Lacey probably looks great in it. In fact, I imagine Lacey looks great in almost any color or style."

Isabel regarded her daughter. "You're right. She does. But don't you think a woman should have more than one pretty dress, especially when she has a good job and the means to pay for one?"

"Mom," Lacey said, sighing in exasperation as she

kicked off her shoes and perched on the edge of the bed. "I just don't need another dress."

"It's not about need, Lacey," Isabel scolded gently, all the love she felt for her daughter in her eyes. "Of course you can make do with one. That isn't the issue. It's about being good to yourself, as good as you are to everyone else." Isabel turned back to Jackson. "I can't tell you how much this young lady has done for me over the years. She even put together the down payment for this shop with money she saved during her residency."

Jackson did a double take. "You saved during your residency?" Most residents—like him—had been on shoestring budgets after a decade or more of scrambling to pay for room, board and tuition. Even with his parents' considerable help and various academic scholarships, it had been a challenge for him to make ends meet. He couldn't fathom how thrifty Lacey must have been.

Lacey regarded her mother gently. "Mom helped put me through college and med school. It was only fair I helped make her dreams come true, too," she said quietly.

"And my dream for a long time has been to own my own bakeshop and live in a small town where people really care about each other. Laramie is that."

"And more." Lacey smiled as she loosened the elastic band holding her honey-blond hair. Lips pursed, she eased her thick silky mane out of the bouncy ponytail on the back of her head.

"But now that we have all that, it's time for us both

to pamper ourselves a little. I have. And I want you to pamper yourself, too, honey."

"Lest you forget, Mom," Lacey shook her hair so it fell about her shoulders in shimmering honey-gold waves, "I already went through that phase my first year as a pediatric resident." Lacey sighed with heartfelt regret. "Spending my time and energy buying new clothes and worrying about how I looked did not make me happy," Lacey said flatly, as she combed her fingers through her hair. "In fact just the opposite happened."

Isabel perched on the edge of the bed. She reached over and patted Lacey's hand. "That's because of the man you were dating, honey."

Now this was getting interesting, Jackson thought, still lounging in the bedroom doorway.

"Quite frankly, honey, Bart's a jerk."

"And then some," Lacey agreed stonily, ignoring Jackson's probing gaze. "But he taught me something important, Mom. Clothes do not make the man or the woman." Lacey cast a look at Jackson's expensive Western shirt and hand-tooled boots. "Sorry, Jackson."

"I admit it. I appreciate fine clothes, fine cars." Fine women. And Lacey Buchanon surely was that.

Eyes sparkling mischievously, Isabel smiled approvingly. "And you look so nice in those clothes, Jackson." Isabel turned back to her daughter. "Doesn't he, Lacey?"

"Yes, Mom," Lacey said wearily, "he does. But that doesn't change things for me. I'm just happier when I don't let material things bog me down."

* * *

"Your mom is right," Jackson said as he and Lacey left the apartment, suitcase and stacks of medical journals in hand. "You should have more than one dress."

"Thanks for the unsolicited advice, Jackson." Lacey waited while he opened the trunk. "But I'm fine the way I am."

"Not exactly." Jackson set the suitcase down, then fit the medical journals in beside it. Lacey tilted her face up to his. Jackson continued affably, "You said it yourself. I appreciate fine clothes. No one's going to believe I'd be seriously interested in a woman with just one dress. With this luncheon coming up, you've got to be outfitted to the nines." It was also yet another way for him to pay her back for her earlier orneriness by insisting she once again do something she didn't want to do.

"I'll be fine," Lacey insisted.

Jackson studied the way she looked in the fading June sunlight. It was the first time he had seen her in any kind of unofficial, nonworking capacity, and he liked what he saw very much. He liked being with her when she didn't have an immediate, work-oriented agenda. Her honey-gold hair had been brushed to a luxurious sheen and was still falling around her face, loose and free. She'd changed out of her scrubs and into a white V-necked T-shirt that hugged her breasts and tiny waist, and a pair of old and faded jeans that did equally impressive things for her hips and thighs. It had been all he could do then and now to keep his hands to himself. "You'll be even finer in a pretty new dress," he told her lazily, determined not to let Lacey get the upper hand in this luncheon situation or anything else. She needed to know if she was going to be with him, he was going to be in charge.

Lacey's chin jutted out stubbornly as she leaned against the trunk. "I will not spend money on something I don't need."

Jackson spread his hands wide. "Then I'll have to buy it for you. Which, come to think of it, may be even better for our purposes."

Lacey rolled her eyes, clearly perturbed. "Of convincing everyone we're involved."

"Or certainly getting there. So come on." He led her around to the front of the car and helped her in.

"Now what?" Lacey said as she watched him fit his tall, rangy body behind the wheel.

"We've got to make a stop before dinner." Jackson waited for a group of high school kids to cross the street, then pulled away from the curb. He drove through the historical downtown area at a leisurely pace, then parked in front of a building at the far end of Main Street. Lockhart's Boutique was written in calligraphy on the front windows. To Jackson's surprise, Lacey was out of the car in a shot, demanding cheerfully, "Why didn't you say this is what you had in mind?"

Jackson followed Lacey into the store. There was a sofa, two arm chairs and a coffee table with a selection of magazines, half of which were geared to men. Hearing the string of bells above the door, Jenna Lockhart breezed out to greet them. "Hey, Lacey."

"Jenna." The two women embraced.

"Jackson!" Jenna turned to him and hugged him, too.

Jackson knew Jenna'd been completely heartbroken when her teenage elopement was circumvented by her boyfriend's wealthy parents. In fact, for a long time her family and friends thought she'd never recover. But she looked great now. Maybe because these days she was putting every drop of energy she had into her work—designing and making clothes.

"I heard you were in town," Jenna continued.

"Got in yesterday," Jackson confirmed.

Jenna looked at the two of them speculatively. "So what brings the two of you in here?"

Jackson sent Lacey an openly amused look designed to send her temper soaring. "Lacey needs a dress and I'm buying."

"No. He's not," Lacey said firmly.

Jackson grinned and continued to regard Lacey with choirboy innocence. "Sure I am. She needs something pretty to wear to a luncheon in my honor."

"And you know Jackson—" Lacey gave Jenna a look and blew out a long and thoroughly exasperated breath "—my navy blue dress just won't do."

"So what have you got?" Jackson asked, looking around with interest at the racks of original dresses, skirts, vests and blouses, all one of a kind, and all created by Jenna, on her sewing machine in the back.

"How about this?" Jenna Lockhart held up something pale yellow, tea length and very very feminine.

"Looks good to me," Jackson murmured.

"To me, too," Lacey said, appreciating the craftsmanship and artistry that had gone into the lace-edged dress. She turned back to Jackson, "But I still can't let you do this."

"Sure you can."

"Let me put it a way you can understand then, Jackson McCabe. Men don't buy me dresses. I buy my own."

Jackson winked. "Then you haven't been dating the right men. Has she, Jenna?"

"Now, you two. Don't put me in the middle of this argument," Jenna said.

"Is that what it is?" Lacey looked at Jackson.

Jackson looked back. "You tell me," he drawled.

After a moment Lacey shrugged. "I suppose you and my mother are right," Lacey said contemplatively, still not dropping her gaze. "It wouldn't kill me to get a new dress every now and then, but I'll pick it out and I'll pay for it."

"If you want to model various selections, I'd be glad to give my opinion," Jackson said.

"No way. Jenna's the designer. Jenna can help me decide."

Jackson shifted uncomfortably in his chair, as he continued to thumb idly through the *Sports Illustrated* on his lap. Lacey was up to something. He knew it.

He'd expected to have to argue her into a dress. Instead she'd capitulated to his demands and had willingly gone off to the backroom with Jenna Lockhart. That had been half an hour ago, and since then he'd heard nothing but low murmurs and riotous laughter. Finally Lacey came out, a garment bag looped over her arm. "Ready?" she said to Jackson cheerfully.

Jackson rolled to his feet, hoping the change in posture would ease the sudden—and very potent—pressure at the front of his jeans. "Don't you want to show me what you bought?" he queried lazily, catching a whiff of her enticing floral perfume.

Lacey smiled, seductive promise in her eyes.

"The first time you're going to see this dress it's going to be on me, not a hanger."

Jenna held the door for both of them. As Lacey passed, she and Lacey exchanged woman-to-woman glances. "Good luck at the luncheon," Jenna murmured in barely checked amusement.

Lacey's green eyes glittered mischievously. "Thanks."

Jackson followed Lacey to the car. He opened the trunk and then draped the garment bag across the rest of her belongings. "You want to drop me at the hospital now?" Lacey asked.

This early? Jackson thought. *No way.* "We're having dinner together first, remember?"

Lacey shrugged, making it clear to Jackson, she didn't want to put much time or effort into that. "We could eat at the hospital cafeteria."

"We could," Jackson conceded affably, still wondering what the heck Jenna and Lacey had been up to back there at Jenna's shop, "but I had in mind somewhere a lot homier."

"Like where?" Lacey prodded, the pulse in her throat suddenly jumping.

Jackson flashed her a deliberately mysterious smile. "That," he murmured seductively, "is for me to know and you to find out."

Chapter 6

"Putt-putt!" Lacey exclaimed as Jackson swaggered up to the ticket booth at the Armadillo Miniature Golf Course and purchased tickets for them both. She turned to him as he handed her a putter and golf ball and ushered her through the gates.

"I should've known you'd pick something competitive," she grumbled as they waited for their turn to enter the Texas-theme course.

Jackson shot a glance at the group of teens in front of them "Afraid you'll lose to me, huh?"

Lacey tossed a look at him over her shoulder. She was determined to come out the victor in this battle of wills if it killed her. "Not much chance of that," she drawled with a sweetly provoking smile. "Unless, of course, I decide to let you win."

Jackson merely grinned as he motioned her ahead to the putting green to begin playing. "Did I ask you to let me win?" He tipped his hat back to better see her face.

"No." Lacey put her ball down on the green and straightened slowly, trying all the while not to notice how his heated gaze tracked her every movement. "But maybe I should for the sake of your ego."

Jackson frowned. "I'd heard that," he murmured mysteriously.

If he was trying to distract her, he was surely doing so, Lacey thought, perturbed, as her first shot took a surprisingly lopsided path down the green, toward the mouth of the giant boot. "Heard what?" she demanded curtly.

"Oh. You know." Jackson shrugged. He gave her a look of choirboy innocence. "Some women still feel like they have a lot to prove…like when it comes to going head-to-head with men." He hit his ball, and to her quickly rising pique, made a hole in one.

Telling herself she had better concentrate, Lacey sauntered down the green, and worked at setting up her next shot. "I have news for you, champ," she said smugly as she hit the ball into the hole with the same accuracy he had just shown. "I've already proven myself in every way I need to prove myself."

Jackson marked down both their scores and followed her onto the next green. He leaned closer, his voice low and sexy in a disturbingly sensual way, "Is that so?"

Lacey tried not to think about the kisses they had already shared. "It is definitely so," she asserted hotly as she matched his shot with a hole in one of her own.

"Hmm." Jackson retrieved both of their golf balls

from the miniature bunkhouse and, peering down at her knowingly, handed her one.

Ignoring the tingling of her fingers where their hands had inadvertently touched, Lacey tightened her fingers around her putter and demanded, "What's that supposed to mean?"

Jackson nodded at her left hand. "I don't see a wedding or engagement ring on your finger."

Despite her decision not to let him get to her, Lacey lifted a brow. "I don't see a wedding ring on yours, either," she volleyed back sweetly.

"Ah," he conceded in a low, sexy voice that said he did indeed have bedrooms and sizzling hot summer nights on his mind, "but I don't want to get married."

No way was she imagining him as her groom, Lacey thought, as she smacked her ball so hard it flew onto the next green causing the group of teens in front of them to giggle uproariously. "Neither do I."

Jackson went to retrieve her ball for her. "Then you prefer hot, lascivious affairs?" he said, returning.

"No, of course not." Lacey blushed as he fit her ball into her fingers.

Jackson leaned his weight on his putter. "Then what do you do about sex?" he asked softly, his gaze roving her face.

A quiver of awareness, that soon turned into a hot, restless tingling, arrowed through her. Ignoring the sudden weakness of her knees, Lacey said, "What do you mean, what do I do about sex?"

"Have you sworn off it?" he regarded her steadily. "Or just never indulged?"

How did he guess these things? Lacey wondered,

as the two of them did a silent dance around the green, with her spinning and turning and reeling back—all on the pretext of setting up her shots—whenever he got the slightest bit close to her. "That, cowboy, is none of your business," Lacey said firmly as she spent the next minute hitting her ball into the center of a silver horseshoe.

Jackson marked down a four next to her name. "I was just curious." He grinned as he made the horseshoe shot in two putts—one of which, Lacey sensed—he had missed on purpose. He wrote down his own score with a cheeky grin. Wreathing his arm about her shoulders, he guided her to the next green. "The bump and grind you did on your way out of the cake, not to mention the stripping, was nothing short of fabulous." He turned slightly, to face her. "Did I mention that?"

Lacey gritted her teeth and ducked out from beneath his grip. "Did I mention I wished you wouldn't?" she returned back lightly.

He stroked his jaw thoughtfully. "So I wondered if you had done it before."

"No." Lacey folded her arms in front of her stoically. "I had not done it before."

Finally he stopped stroking his jaw, dropped his hand to his side and said, "Hmm. You showed a re-markable talent."

Lacey rolled her eyes and went back to playing putt-putt. "I'm a quick study, always have been." This time she made a hole in one.

This time Jackson missed. "You just choose not to study sex."

Lacey watched him line up another shot and make

it with ease. She propped her hand on her hip. "Why do you insist on talking about this?"

Jackson chuckled as he escorted her to the next hole. "Why do you insist we not?"

Lacey missed another shot. "Because," she hissed self-consciously as she once again tried to line up a shot into the mouth of the longhorn cow, "it is embarrassing me!"

Jackson hit his own ball in. "Sex makes you uncomfortable?"

What could she say to that? Lacey wondered miserably. That she was woefully inexperienced? That even when she had become close to getting engaged to Bart, she hadn't been brave enough to let herself be vulnerable enough to actually—Lacey swallowed and cut off her line of thought. She most definitely did not need to be thinking about that! Never mind in conjunction with a ladies' man like Jackson McCabe! She led the way to the next hole. "Your shot."

Jackson's mood turned abruptly solemn as he strolled toward her with easy, sensual grace. "So it is."

Lacey watched in frustration as he held his putter in both capable hands and made yet another perfect hole in one, landing his ball right into the bed of the miniature pickup truck. Darn it all, he was beating her, and all because he was unnerving her with all this talk about her sex life. Which no doubt was the plan. Fortunately she was just as capable as he at turning the tables.

She led the way to the next hole. "So, cowboy, now that we've dissected mine, let's talk about your sex life."

Jackson grinned, stuck his thumbs through the belt loops on either side of his fly. Regaining his arrogant stance, he regarded her sassily and asked, "What do you want to know?"

Everything, Lacey thought, as she tore her eyes from his brawny forearms and turned away, blushing. But that didn't mean she should. So what if he made her feel more a woman with a few kisses than any other man ever had? It didn't mean they had anything special, she told herself firmly as she missed another shot. It just meant they had some chemistry. She didn't have to give in to his lazy charm and boundless enthusiasm.

Lacey lined up a second shot, and landed her ball beneath the raised horse-shoe-clad foot of a bucking bronco. "What are you doing about sex these days?"

He held her eyes with his mesmerizing sea-blue gaze, making her feel even more hot-and-bothered inside. "This week or last?"

Once again she had the strong sensation he wanted to kiss her. Senses reeling, she stepped back. "Is there a difference?" she quipped dryly, shooting him a drop-dead look

"Oh, yeah." His smile bloomed slowly as his unrepentent eyes remained trained on hers. "A big one."

"I see." Light-headed from the images crowding her thoughts, Lacey drew a deep breath and stepped back. She angled her head back to better see his face, and the mirth she saw there gave her the strength she needed to put him in his place. "This week—now that you're back in Laramie—you're doing without, and last week when you were still in Forth Worth, you weren't."

Jackson grinned, even more unrepentently, as he

made another hole in one, and then—as darkness fell around them and the teens playing in front of them got even further ahead—escorted her to the next hole. "I think you've got it a little backward," he drawled.

Lacey stifled a moan of sheer misery and tearing her eyes from his wind-tossed hair, studied the layout of the next putting green with more-than-necessary care. "What do you mean?"

Jackson took the putter out of her hands, backed her up against the side of the faux waterfall and clamped both his strong arms around her, anchoring one at her waist, the other at her neck. "Last week I had absolutely zero romance in my life," he said softly, nuzzling her neck. "And this week—"

"Jackson…!" Lacey shoved with all her might-to no avail.

"Lacey…!" Grinning, he mocked her whispered indignation. Then all was lost as his lips came down on hers, stifling her gasp of moral outrage and delivering a steamy kiss. Trembling from the sweet pressure of his lips on hers and the thrill that went with his kiss, Lacey released another muffled gasp of protest, and then all was lost as he dominated her lips with the passion she had ached to explore again. For the first time in her life, she was with a man who didn't hesitate to give her the complete physicality she craved, and she reveled in it. She reveled in the hard, insistent pressure of his mouth over hers and the demanding sweep of his tongue. She moaned and sagged against him. Wanting. Needing. Letting her arms come up to hold him closer, instead of pushing him away, and that was when they heard it, the sound of low laughter somewhere to their left.

It was the group of teens who had been playing in front of them. Lacey recognized some of the kids from the local high school. One of the girls elbowed her boyfriend. "And you said she didn't know what she was talking about when she gave that sex talk over at the high school last month. Obviously she does! They both do!"

The heat of shame filled Lacey's face. She couldn't believe it. She was a physician in this town. She was supposed to set an example for the children she treated. And instead, she and Jackson had been acting like two hormone-driven teenagers with absolutely no common sense!

"Didn't mean to be a distraction to y'all," Jackson murmured.

Although, Lacey noted irately, he didn't seem to mind being caught kissing her like there was no tomorrow!

"No problem!" one of the teenage boys murmured back, casting Jackson an admiring glance. "We liked the show just fine!"

"Yeah!" One of the other boys threw in. "Maybe later you could stop by the gym and give us guys some pointers," one of the boys told Jackson with no small amount of hero worship. "'Cause I gotta tell you, Doc McCabe. My gal, Sally, never melts against me the way Doc Buchanon was melting against you!"

It took another three minutes of banter, but Jackson finally got rid of the group of teens playing ahead of them. Unfortunately by then there was another group behind them, as well, who were equally as interested in the goings-on, so Jackson waved them on ahead, too, on the pretext that he and Lacey needed to stop and get something to eat in the Armadillo snack bar. "You're trying to cause a scandal," Lacey huffed as they sat down to their "dinner" of chili dogs, fries and cold drinks. Hoping to make herself undesirable in the kissing department for the rest of the evening, she had heaped on the onions, only to see him chuckle and do the same.

"So what if I am?" Jackson asked as he added extra mustard to his chili dog, too.

"I'll tell you what!" Lacey said as she took a bite of the delicious cheese, chili and onion-topped treat, then dabbed the corners of her mouth with her napkin. "When you leave Laramie and go off to take that job in Fort Worth, I still have to live here, Jackson McCabe!"

Jackson chowed down his chili dog and regarded her in thoughtful silence. "I'd buy that," he drawled finally, "if you hadn't jumped out of a cake, stripped down to one very sexy gold lamé bikini, sprinted me away to a private office and lassoed me to a chair, all just to get me to pay attention to you."

"Okay, so I don't really care about what people say about me." Lacey scowled as she dipped her French fry in ketchup. "But I don't want you feigning desire just to throw off my putt-putt game."

Jackson took a long drink of his soda and stared at her over the rim of his paper cup. "Is that what you think I was doing?"

Lacey flushed, knowing from the pressure at the

front of his jeans when he'd kissed her and held her close that his desire for her had been very real. As real as hers for him! Deciding to ignore what she couldn't discuss, she plucked the putt-putt score pad out of his shirt pocket and tossed it down on the table between them. "Look at these scores!" She tapped the half-filled-out white card with the end of her finger. "There is absolutely no denying your constant moves on me worked to thoroughly distract me from my game!"

Jackson's grin was suddenly very sexy and very pleased. "Now who's being competitive?" he teased, letting the straw rest against his sensuous lower lip.

Another wave of heat swept through Lacey's cheeks. "You know what I mean," she said grumpily, wishing he had chosen to sit on the opposite side of the picnic table instead of on the bench right next to her.

Turning so his legs straddled the picnic bench and he was facing her, Jackson said with a cocky grin, "So you admit it makes you nervous to talk about sex."

"It makes me edgy," Lacey corrected in a huff, very much aware they were the only two in the snack-bar area, as everyone else was out on the course. "When you and I talk about it, yes!"

"And why is that?" he taunted boldly, his heated gaze slowly roving her face before fastening ever so deliberately on her mouth.

Lacey rolled her eyes and went back to eating her French fries very slowly and with a great deal more concentration than was needed. "Because we shouldn't be discussing it, that's why!"

Jackson shrugged. One forearm slung across his thigh, he leaned even closer and whispered in her ear,

"Why not, when we've already established that neither of us wants to get married, haven't sworn off sex
and have found—much to your chagrin—considerable
chemistry between us."

Hoping it would ease her parched throat, Lacey took
another long sip of soda. Sitting up straight, she forced
herself to meet his gaze. "You mean you don't mind
the fact you're attracted to me."

Jackson laid a hand across his heart. "Honey, I don't
mind anything that gets my heart rate up into the target
zone and makes me feel this way."

Lacey sat back, pulling her upper body even farther
away from his. "And how is that?" she queried drolly.

"Warm and tingling." Jackson waggled his eyebrows
teasingly at her. He took her hand in his and turned it
over so it lay against the hard, heated surface of his
blue-jeaned thigh, then fit his palm over it. "How does
this make you feel?" he asked softly.

Exactly the same, times one hundred, Lacey thought
wistfully, but there was no way on this green earth she
was letting him know that! Lacey crumpled up her
paper napkin and tossed it down between them. She
glared at him, sparing nothing. "I mean it, Jackson,"
she told him stonily, vaulting to her feet. Her hands
clenched at her sides. "I don't want you feigning desire
for me."

Jackson shrugged his broad shoulders restlessly and
stayed where he was. "Who's feigning?"

The next thing Lacey knew she was sprawled across
Jackson's lap. He had her in his arms and was delivering another long, slow, incredibly sexy kiss. He gave
her no quarter; she said, To heck with it, and gave

him none back. It was all hot, searing need. He kissed her with a sweetness and a tenderness she had never guessed he possessed, and then—as before—he slowly let her go.

Lacey was even more breathless when they drew apart. Whole body trembling, she tried to get her bearings. "So you see, I do desire you and you desire me," Jackson said, ignoring the muted tittering of the teens in the distance. He touched his hand to her face, tilting her head up to his. "And since we feel that way—"

Lacey's laugh was shaky. "You want us to follow this to its natural conclusion and have an affair," she guessed, not sure why this surprised her, only knowing that it did.

"Why not?" Jackson asked earnestly. As if he were doing them both a favor!

Lacey shoved away from him and vaulted off his lap. Grabbing her trash, she headed for the green plastic bin. "Sorry," she said as Jackson strode after her, just as determinedly. "I don't have flings with men who are only looking to pass the time while they're on vacation."

"Why not?" Jackson tossed his trash away, too, and went back to get their putters and balls so they could finish their game. "We're both adults. We know what the score is."

"Exactly why I won't do it," Lacey stormed as she marched back to complete the eighteen hole miniature golf course as if nothing of importance had happened after all. She shot him one last quelling look. "I'm not going to be your pastime, or anyone else's, either, Jackson McCabe!"

* * *

"Since when did you become the town playboy?" Lilah demanded over breakfast the next morning.

Since last night, Jackson thought. The truth was he didn't know what had come over him, either. It wasn't like him to put the moves on a woman in public, never mind a woman he'd just met, a woman he wasn't completely sure he even liked or could ever get along with on a personal level. And yet, despite that, he had felt an overpowering urge to stake a claim, to let every other man in town know to back off because he was making a move for Lacey now. And he had known that kissing her in public, putting on the full-court press, would do just that. And then there had been the added bonus of rattling Dr. Know-it-all just a tad, of seeing the blush come into her cheeks, and the sparkle in her eyes. There had been something so right about feeling her melt against him and mold her lips to his, that he'd had to do it again. And if truth be told, he wanted to do it again even more.

But not in public. No, next time would be private, he promised himself firmly as he cut into Lilah's famous huevos rancheros. The next time would be just for the two of them.

"It's all over town this morning. Honestly, couldn't the two of you have found someplace to neck besides the Armadillo putt-putt golf course!" Lilah continued, completely exasperated.

Now, there was an idea, Jackson mused, adding even more picante sauce to his eggs. There were plenty of places the two of them could go. Nice, quiet, romantic places where they could kiss as long—and often and heatedly—as they liked. Now, wouldn't that be something!

"Your mother and I both care about that young woman," John reminded Jackson.

"I have no intention of hurting her," Jackson said, looking at both Lilah and John.

"Well, I don't want you seducing her and then leaving town, either," Lilah fumed as she poured a steaming mug of coffee and set it next to his plate.

Jackson couldn't imagine making love to Lacey and then walking away, either. "I won't hurt her, Mom. I promise," he said quietly.

"Does that mean you won't seduce her into having an affair?" Lilah demanded.

It means, Jackson thought, *that I won't do anything she doesn't want to do.* He had the idea, after last night, that Lacey was as hot for him as he was for her. And Lord knew that didn't happen often in this lifetime. In fact, he couldn't think of one time in his life where he'd felt the way he'd felt last night. Even his experience with Amelia—badly as that had ended—hadn't begun to compare.

"Lilah, leave the boy alone." John exhaled wearily and gave Jackson a man-to-man look before turning back to his wife. "We've taught him well and brought him up right. He knows the difference between right and wrong. Don't you, son? And hurting Lacey would be about the most wrong-headed thing a man could do around here."

Jackson pushed away from the table, the guilt assailing him doing nothing to negate the desire he felt or the fierce desire to possess. "I won't hurt her," he promised gruffly. That was the last thing he wanted to do. "And that's a promise."

He wasn't promising he wouldn't make love to the honey-haired, green-eyed Lacey. Because that, he feared, was a promise he would never be able to keep.

"I really am better, aren't I, Dr. Lacey?" Molly Weatherby asked as Lacey finished examining her, shortly after lunchtime.

"It would appear so, honey." Lacey smiled. Molly's fever had broken during the night and hadn't returned. The pain in her tummy had disappeared, as had the persistent nausea and vomiting. In fact, she was tolerating liquids by mouth so well they'd been able to remove the IV and start her back on soft foods. She still looked pretty wiped out, but that was to be expected after being as sick as she had been the past few days.

"Does this mean she'll be released from the hospital today?" Patricia Weatherby asked anxiously.

Lacey nodded, then warned, "But Molly is still going to have to take it easy for a few days, just to be on the safe side."

Patricia Weatherby looked worried again. "Are you sure your mother is okay with the two of us staying with her?"

"Absolutely," Lacey reassured her. "In fact, she's got the guest room all ready for the two of you. And she wants Teddy Beddy—" Lacey tweaked the nose of Molly's favorite stuffed animal "—to come stay with her, too."

* * *

"I heard Molly Weatherby was just released," Jackson said, when he ran into Lacey in the hallway outside the E.R. at the end of the day.

Lacey nodded and filled him in on all the latest test results and pertinent medical details. "Everything looks good but her white count, which is still a little high—ten thousand five hundred."

"What was it yesterday?" Jackson asked.

"A little bit above eleven thousand. It was thirteen thousand when she was admitted."

"At least it's going in the right direction," Jackson said.

Lacey nodded. Both of them knew the count might stay high for a few days, while Molly recovered from her illness. And that that in itself was nothing unusual.

"So what are you thinking," Jackson asked casually, "that it was just a nasty case of gastroenteritis?"

Lacey nodded. "Looks that way now. But I'll feel better in a few days—when she starts looking a little better and not so wiped-out." Until then, there were still things that could go wrong. And Lacey knew she wouldn't feel she could relax her vigilance until Molly was one hundred percent recuperated. Which was another reason why she was glad she was able to talk the Weatherbys into staying with her mother. This way, it would be easy to keep a close eye on little Molly, as well as lend a helping hand to Patricia.

Lacey glanced down at Jackson's scrubs. Damned if he didn't look handsome as all get-out in surgical blue. "Did you get called again?" she asked curiously, happier than ever she'd managed to talk him into pinch-hitting in surgery while he was around.

Jackson nodded. "I'm headed up to the O.R., to do a hot gall bladder now, but I'm free later. If you've got time, maybe we could have some dinner together later tonight."

"Sorry, I'm booked. I've got Seth Schofield coming in for an interview in a few minutes. I'm going to show him around Laramie tonight, and he'll meet with the rest of the hospital board and staff tomorrow for a formal interview." Lacey studied Jackson's less-than happy expression. "Your dad said you might know him."

Jackson nodded, appearing more displeased by the moment. "Oh, yeah, I know him all right. We went to med school together."

Lacey moved out of the way of a gurney coming through and waited for Jackson to continue. When he didn't, she spread her hands. "And…?"

To Lacey's frustration, Jackson volleyed back with a question of his own. "How long has this been lined up?"

Lacey lifted her shoulders in an elegant shrug. "Since thirty minutes after you nixed the idea of working here on any permanent basis." She paused as the P.A. system paged another doctor, then tilted her head up to his and continued, "He was next on the short list of surgeons interested in living and working here." Lacey studied the conflicted expression in Jackson's sea blue eyes. "Does this bother you?" And if it did, what did it mean?

It bothered him a lot, Jackson thought, though he

knew he had no reason to feel jealous. After all he didn't want the position at Laramie Community. And they did need a good surgeon on staff, or two or three, to serve, not just Laramie, but the surrounding county.

"Not at all," Jackson replied smoothly, aware Lacey was still waiting for his reaction. "Seth's a good guy. Just…" Jackson paused.

"What?"

Jackson shrugged. He felt it only fair to warn her. "I'm not sure he would like it here. He grew up in the city."

"So did I, and I like it here so much I plan to live the rest of my life here." Lacey paused, her eyes never leaving his face. "In fact, I got the feeling from talking to Seth that he was just like me in that regard."

Jackson spread his hands and told himself it was none of his business, anyway. "Then I hope it goes well for you," he heard himself say.

Lacey smiled. "I do, too."

"Jackson! I thought I caught a glimpse of you earlier when Lacey and I were touring the hospital," Seth Schofield said when Jackson caught up with them later that evening in the Wagon Wheel Restaurant & Grill.

"And then again when we were driving by the schools and parks," Lacey added dryly, looking at him as if she knew darn well that his shadowing them hadn't exactly been an accident.

Jackson accepted Seth's ready invitation and pulled up a chair at the square, wooden table. "That's the problem with Laramie," Jackson lamented, not shy at all about getting his message across to Seth, figuring it was better to be straight with him now than later, and hence discourage him. "It's so small you can't help but run into one another. And the night life, well, let's just say it's practically nonexistent." The waitress took his order for a glass of iced tea.

"That's right. You're from here, aren't you?" Seth asked Jackson.

Lacey, who'd just about finished her own dinner of chicken-fried steak, mashed potatoes and green beans, jumped in before Jackson could further delineate what he perceived to be Laramie's flaws. Smiling warmly at Seth, she said, "Jackson's parents actually started the hospital years ago. His dad, John, is a family practitioner, and he delivered most of the kids who are now our age," Lacey said, "including Jackson and his brothers, from what I hear."

"Really," Seth said, impressed. He looked at Jackson, all too ready to compete against him head-to-head if necessary. "Are you in the running for this job, too?"

Not sure how he felt about the fact that he had been taken out of the running as abruptly and unfairly as he'd been put in, Jackson shook his head.

"Because Jackson was a local golden boy, he was the hospital's first choice," Lacey added, her continuing disappointment about that clear. "He turned it down," she continued with a forced smile.

Seth eyed Jackson curiously, then sopped up the last of the cream gravy on his plate with a flaky, golden-brown biscuit. "Guess it's not surprising," Seth drawled, for a moment looking more like someone who had just stepped out of a fashion magazine than the kind of rough-and-tumble, ready-for-anything, fly-by-the-seat-of-his-pants surgeon a small city like Laramie would require. "Given the fact whoever takes the job will likely be the hospital's only surgeon, there really isn't enough competition here to keep you interested, is there?"

Jackson had initially thought that. Now, after being there just a few days, and being challenged to do his best without having access to the state-of-the-art equipment he'd gotten used to during his residency, he wasn't sure that was the case. The truth was, a lot more needed to be done to upgrade the surgery department—if you could even call it that—at Laramie Community Hospital. And it would take a real mover and a shaker to make it happen. Jackson wasn't sure Seth had it in him to do all the wheedling, begging and cajoling it was going to take to raise the kind of big money that would accomplish that. But there was no reason Seth—or Lacey—needed to know that, Jackson thought. Especially when all Seth was really asking was why Jackson had turned down the Laramie job in favor of another in Fort Worth.

"I admit I've got a hankering to be the best," Jackson said.

"Me, too," Seth parried back lightly as he balled up his linen napkin and dropped it beside his plate. "But then you know that, don't you?"

"Mind letting me in on the secret?" Lacey asked.

Jackson looked at Lacey. "Seth and I competed for some of the same slots all through med school and residency," he said casually.

"Sometimes I would come out ahead," Seth explained. "Sometimes Jackson would." The corners of

Seth's mouth turned up ruefully. "So it's funny that I would end up considering a job he's already turned down."

Not really, Jackson thought. "You must have had your pick of offers, just like me."

"I did, and do. But this is the one I find most interesting to date." Seth smiled at Lacey…with a level of appreciation Jackson found totally inappropriate under the circumstances. "Lacey's done a great job of showing me around."

As Seth continued to smile at Lacey, Jackson's pique increased. He didn't know why; it wasn't really his business. Lacey wasn't really his woman—she was just pretending to be—but it irked the heck out of him to see Seth Schofield trying to charm Lacey. He was even acting a bit as if he was a date and not a person she was being forced, by virture of the fact she was chairman of the search committee for a new surgeon, to show Seth around town.

Jackson thanked the waitress for his iced tea. As soon as she'd left, Lacey turned her attention back to Seth. "Speaking of showing you around," she told him, smiling graciously, "there's not a lot of night life in Laramie, but there is a movie theater, a country-and-western dance hall and a putt-putt golf course, not to mention a knockout park with a really great trail for hiking and biking. Any of that interest you?"

"Actually," Seth said, pushing away from his plate, "I think I'd like to go for a run. Clear my head. Think about the questions I'm likely to be asked tomorrow and the ones I'd like to ask in return."

Lacey smiled. "If you change your mind, I'll be at

the hospital. I'm bunking down in an on-call room for now."

Seth paused. "Any particular reason?"

Lacey shook her head. "Long story. Bottom line is it's convenient."

The bottom line was, Jackson thought, Lacey's mother was right. Lacey did sacrifice far too much for others and do too little for herself. That, he thought, was something that could—and should—be changed. Not surprisingly, Lacey walked Seth as far as the restaurant door and said her goodbyes to him in private. Again it took far too long. Finally Seth left and Lacey came back to wait for the check. All too happy about the way this had turned out, Jackson slouched in his chair and drawled, "Well. Looks like you've got some time on your hands tonight after all!"

Lacey glared at Jackson. "Don't count on it."

Chapter 7

"Feeling a little jealous this evening, Jackson?" Lacey asked as she collected the check, put a tip on the table and headed for the door. "Or is it just plain competitive?"

She stopped and paid the check at the cash register, then swept out the door. Jackson grabbed his Stetson from the rack by the door. Setting it squarely on his head, he followed, his steps deceptively lazy as he fell in beside her.

Ignoring the sexy masculine fragrance of soap and aftershave clinging to his skin, Lacey slanted a glance at his ruggedly handsome face and continued sweetly, "Or is it sort of an ex-girlfriend type of thing—you don't want her, but you don't want anyone else to have her, either—that you're feeling about this position at the hospital?"

"Hey!" Jackson slapped both his hands dramatically

across his chest. "I was just waiting for your business to be done so I could save you from sleeping at the hospital tonight." Lacey rolled her eyes in exasperation and marched on ahead, her sneaker-clad feet moving soundlessly across the sidewalk.

His manner, as unperturbed as hers, was fiery; he sauntered closer to her side as she stalked down Main Street toward the hospital.

Jackson caught her elbow in a gentle but implacable grip as they approached the first crosswalk. As they waited for the light to change and the traffic to pass, he turned his head down to hers. He looked sexy and approachable in an unutterably masculine way, and she felt a lightning-bolt surge of attraction.

The only problem was she didn't want to feel that way about him.

Sea-blue eyes glittering warmly, he murmured, "I think you should move out to my family's ranch for the next couple of days."

"You do," Lacey replied dryly.

"Yes." His sexy smile widened. "I do. After all, we've got plenty of room. And plenty of food. And it'd sure be a lot more comfortable than staying in the on-call quarters."

It was a tempting invitation, and if she hadn't been so attracted to him, and so angry with him for interfering in her life and her business just now, she might have taken him up on his offer. But she was angry with him, Lacey reminded herself sternly, and she was attracted to him—hopelessly so!—and she would do well to remember that before she got any more involved with him.

Pointedly she removed his hand from her elbow and pivoted to face him. "What do your parents think about this?" she demanded, slapping both hands on her hips.

His eyes swept up the length of her jeans and the pale peach Isabel's Bakeshop T-shirt to her face. "They suggested it before I could even bring it up."

That didn't surprise Lacey. John and Lilah McCabe had always been generous. But it did sort of surprise her about Jackson. Thus far he'd struck her as the guy who always had one foot out the door. And that being the case, it'd be wise if she kept her distance. "Thanks, but I'll be fine at the hospital."

"Sure?" Jackson asked with a provoking grin as the light changed and they headed across the street to the next block. "We could go riding before sunrise. You haven't experienced Laramie to its fullest until you've seen a Texas sunrise on the McCabe ranch."

That was a tempting offer, Lacey thought, as they strolled past the drugstore and the red-and-white pole of the old-fashioned barbershop. It had been ages since she'd done anything that frivolously romantic.

Which was, perhaps, what the sexy bounder was counting on. "Nah," Lacey said, as her customary common sense promptly reasserted itself. She tucked her fingers in the front pockets of her favorite jeans. "I'd just be tempted to try to talk you into accepting the position at the hospital again."

Jackson tilted his hat back and considered her. "I thought you wanted Seth Schofield for that now."

But Seth hadn't been—and still wasn't—her first choice, Lacey thought, as they stopped at yet another crosswalk and she glanced up into his eyes. Aware

Jackson was still studying her carefully, Lacey swallowed hard around the tension gathering in her throat and shrugged. "I haven't recruited him yet."

"But he seemed interested," Jackson persisted, almost too casually.

Hand pressed lightly against her back, he guided her safely across the street.

Lacey shrugged and worked hard to keep her own emotions in check. "Like you, he also has a lot of offers," she murmured. "He can probably write his own ticket." Her pulse racing, she stepped away from the tingling warmth of his hand. "Unlike you, he's at least giving Laramie a hard look."

Jackson's gaze fastened on her lips. "We could go riding without talking about the job."

What would be the point? Lacey thought despairingly. Jackson was leaving for the kind of life that would never make her happy in a million years. She smiled at him sadly. "I don't think so."

Jackson scowled. "Meaning what—that the only reason you'd go riding with me is to fulfill some sort of agenda?" he snapped, his boots smacking against the concrete.

There were other reasons, like the way he made her feel whenever he was around, but those were reasons he didn't need to know about. All too willing to use whatever it took to wedge some distance between them, Lacey said, "That upsets you? That I have a purpose here, bringing quality medical care to the community and that I'm willing to expend a lot of time and energy on it?"

The grooves around his mouth deepened as he

pressed his lips together. He continued to regard her with a steady, analyzing look as they reached the hospital parking lot. "Is that the only reason you kissed me?" he demanded, angling even closer.

The heat of a flush climbed from her neck to her face. Even standing out there in the midst of a very public place with him, she felt ridiculously exposed, vulnerable. She propped her hands on her hips, wanting only to flee. "I kissed you because you hauled me into your arms and locked your lips over mine!" She started to step past.

He moved, barring her way, not about to let her go until they had finished their discussion. "But you didn't have to kiss me back!" he pointed out angrily.

That wasn't the way she remembered it, Lacey thought. The moment he'd taken her in his arms and locked his lips over hers the whole world had stopped. It had been just the two of them. And in many ways, still was. Her chin tautening at the implacable note she heard in his voice, Lacey reminded him just how persuasive and deliberate he had been in his conquest of her.

"I don't think that I had much choice, cowboy."

A muscle worked in his jaw; derision glowed in his eyes. "You had a choice."

Yes, Lacey admitted reluctantly to herself, aware her neck and shoulders were already drawn tight as a bow. She had a choice. And she'd chosen to succumb, however briefly, not for any ulterior motive, but because Jackson had made her feel like no other man ever had. She had kissed him back and delighted in it because deep down she had wanted to be with him, for however long he was in town.

She knew exactly how foolish that made her. But she wasn't foolish enough to tell him any of that. Bitter experience had taught her to guard her heart around men like Jackson.

She sighed, then drew in another bolstering breath. "So I crossed the line a bit, to get your attention," she fibbed with all the insouciance she could muster, forcing herself to meet his probing sea-blue eyes all the while. "What's the big deal?"

Jackson fixed her with a cool stare and didn't answer.

Without another word he walked away.

"What happened between you and my son last night?" Lilah McCabe asked the next morning when she happened to pass Lacey in the hall at the hospital. "He came home in such a mood!"

He'd left her in such a mood! Lacey thought, perversely glad that Jackson apparently wasn't any happier about the acrimonious way they'd parted company in the hospital parking lot than she was. Wanting to keep the nature of their argument private, Lacey countered Lilah's question with one of her own. "Is that unusual?" Lacey asked Lilah, as she stepped aside to let an orderly and wheelchair-bound patient pass. "For Jackson to be in a mood?"

"Actually, yes." Her bright blue eyes glowing affectionately, Lilah shifted the stack of patient charts she was carrying to her other arm. "Jackson is rather used to getting his way in life."

If that wasn't the understatement of the year! "So I've noticed," Lacey said dryly.

Lilah's silvery-blond hair bobbed around her face as she regarded Lacey fondly. "But not with you—"

Lacey shrugged, aware if she wasn't careful she really was going to be wearing her heart on her sleeve. "Golden boys aren't really my type."

Lilah's smile deepened knowingly. "Really. I would've thought from the sparks flying whenever the two of you are around each other that Jackson was exactly your type."

Lacey blushed and, unable to deny the chemistry between herself and Lilah's son, said with no small amount of embarrassment, "I haven't exactly got a stellar track record in the romance department."

"Neither has Jackson, if you want to know the truth," Lilah confided softly. "Which is perhaps why—" Lilah stopped and bit her lip.

Why what? Lacey wondered, thwarted. "Tell me you're going to finish that sentence," she moaned theatrically, knowing her curiosity about Jackson McCabe knew no bounds.

Lilah shook her head as another nurse passed. "I really shouldn't. Jackson would kill me if he knew I'd even brought up— Well, we're just lucky the two of them didn't get engaged. Although I'm not sure Jackson saw it that way then or now. Maybe if he did, he'd feel free to pursue someone else. Someone like you, Lacey."

"He's been pursuing me," Lacey replied plaintively, not sure how she felt about the knowledge that Jackson had indeed been serious about a woman once. The truth was that just the idea of Jackson with another woman made her jealous. And she was not the jealous type, never had been.

Lilah sighed, shook her head and continued firmly. "He's got to put that—put her—behind him, or he's never going to be able to go on with his life."

Jackson spent the morning doing two emergency surgeries back to back. He had a third scheduled for later in the afternoon, plus appointments with four more patients who had requested he do their surgeries since he was in town and temporarily on staff at the hospital. He supposed he should have minded—this was to be his vacation before beginning work with the practice in Fort Worth—but the truth was he was rather enjoying helping the people he had known growing up in Laramie. He was enjoying being on staff at Laramie Community Hospital. Although, Jackson noted, looking at the wish list he'd drawn up for the operating room, there was still a lot needed in the way of equipment there, and he planned to do what he could to get it for them after he arrived in Fort Worth. Perhaps some wealthy benefactor could be found to underwrite more investment in the hospital.

Meanwhile, he had to decide where he was going to live when he moved there. Jackson sighed, looking at the tall stack of Fort Worth real estate brochures. Problem was, he couldn't really seem to get interested in finding a place. Hell, he didn't even know if he wanted an apartment or condo or house, which made it pretty hard to narrow anything down.

Lacey rapped on the open doorway and stuck her

head into the small office adjacent to the recovery room where Jackson was sitting. As she studied him briefly, her teeth raked across the pouty softness of her lower lip. "I heard you were in here dictating some post-op notes. Still at it?"

Jackson shook his head and let his gaze rove the flushed contours of her pretty, heart-shaped face. It was the first time he'd seen her all day, and he was hungry for the sight of her—maybe more so than he should have been, considering the way they had parted the previous evening. Nevertheless, she was here now and he couldn't take his eyes off her. She was wearing her usual hospital attire of green scrubs and white lab coat embroidered with her name, her stethoscope looped around her neck. But instead of the bouncy ponytail she'd worn the previous couple of days, today she had drawn her hair into some sort of complicated braid. The pink of summer heat tinged her high, delicately sculpted cheeks, and her skin appeared flawless in the sunlight pouring in through the windows.

"I'm finished," Jackson told her, pointing to the closed patient files beneath the dictating equipment in front of him.

"Great!" Needing no further invitation, it seemed, Lacey bounded the rest of the way in. She was carrying a paper sack and two cold drinks, and immediately set them out on the desk. "I heard how hard you've been working this morning, so I brought you lunch." She shrugged. "Part of our deal, you know. You help me out—I mean the hospital—and I do stuff for you."

Jackson recalled their deal. All too well. Perversely, he'd hoped she'd been doing this just for him, to make up for what she'd said, for what he'd hoped was not true, the previous night. Guess not, he thought, determined not to let her see how discouraged he felt to realize this, too, was all still part and parcel of her "agenda."

"You're too kind," Jackson said wryly, opening the sandwich she handed him. Layers of thinly sliced rare roast beef, with Monterey pepper jack cheese, lettuce, tomato, brown mustard and jalapeños on pumpernickel rye bread. His favorite. How had she known? "You've been talking to someone if you know about this," he told her.

Lacey nodded as she unwrapped her own ham and cheese. "Which brings me to my next point," Lacey murmured, watching as he bit down on the spicy delicious sandwich. Her pretty green eyes lasered in on his. "Who was she, Jackson?"

Jackson blinked. "Who's who?" he asked, not following.

Lacey popped the top on her can of cola. Meeting his glance equably, she continued softly, "The woman you wanted to ask to marry you but didn't."

Jackson choked at her directness. This he definitely had not expected. Briefly he put a fist to his lips and struggled to regain his composure. "Who told you about that?"

Lacey shrugged. "It's not important."

Jackson snorted. "Like hell it's not! Not that I even have to ask," he continued furiously when it looked as if Lacey was not about to spill all to him then and there. "There's only one person who could know about that—" he began, setting the trap.

Lacey held up both hands, stopping him mid-tirade. "Jackson, don't." She leaned forward earnestly. "Your mother meant well."

Jackson swore silently to himself. "My mom told you this?"

"Wait a minute!" Lacey put her own sandwich down without taking a bite. Pink color filled her cheeks and outrage sparkled in her light green eyes. "You said you knew!"

Jackson acknowledged his guilt with a slight tilt to his head. "So I fudged a little," he admitted.

"A little!" Lacey fumed. "Now you're going to get me in trouble!"

"No," Jackson corrected with exaggerated patience as he slowly rolled to his feet. It was just these kinds of violations of his privacy that made him not want to return to Laramie to live. "I'm going to get my mother in trouble." He loved his mother dearly, but that did not mean he was going to let her meddle in his private life, even a little bit.

Lacey jumped up and raced ahead of him to the door. "You can't." She put her hands on the door frame on either side of her, trying to bar his exit.

His patience wearing quickly, Jackson propped his hands on his hips and stared down at her. He wished she didn't look so damned beautiful. And that he didn't desire her so much. "Why not?"

Lacey's chin jutted out stubbornly. "Because I won't let you."

Jackson shook his head. "You won't let me?" he echoed incredulously.

Lacey swallowed, finally becoming aware, Jackson

guessed, that she was in a most vulnerable position with her arms spread on either side of her, her head tilted back, looking up at him. It was all he could do not to step forward and take her in his arms and deliver another long, hot, steamy kiss that ended this entire discussion once and for all, here and now.

"Is it true?" Lacey persisted, softly but determinedly.

"Were you in love with someone who treated you badly? Is she the reason you're not interested in getting married, why you only want to play the field?"

Figuring this was one conversation best not overheard by anyone linked to the hospital grapevine, lest it be all over Laramie lickety-split, Jackson hooked an arm around Lacey's waist, guided her forward and shut the door behind her. "I never said I wouldn't marry," he corrected gruffly.

Lacey wiggled free of him and went back to her chair and her lunch. "Well," she huffed, as she got comfortable once again, "Your mother certainly thinks that's the case."

Jackson rolled his eyes and grudgingly offered his assessment of the situation. "She's just upset I was stupid enough to get myself in a position where I could be hurt," he grumbled.

Lacey lifted her can of cola to her lips. "What happened?"

Jackson settled down to finish his sandwich, too. "It's the oldest story in the world."

"That may be but I haven't heard it yet."

Jackson said nothing.

"Look, you don't have to tell me if you don't want

to," Lacey said as she picked up her sandwich once again. Her eyes pinning his, she added softly, "But I'd really like it if you would."

Maybe it would be cathartic to talk to someone about it, Jackson mused. Heaven knew it hadn't helped to keep everything bottled up inside. Figuring finally it might as well be him satisfying Lacey's considerable curiosity rather than anyone else, Jackson blew out a long weary breath and said, "I met Amelia at a party my last year of med school. She was just twenty-five, but she was already a superb businesswoman and gourmet chef in her own right. And when she looked at me, it was like I was the only guy in the entire universe for her." At the time it hadn't felt like an ego thing, but looking back, Jackson knew that had been at least part of it.

"That must have been wonderful for you," she said softly.

Jackson shrugged. "It would've been if our love for each other had been real."

"But it wasn't," Lacey guessed sadly.

"No." Jackson's shoulders tensed as he forced himself to be unflinchingly honest. "She wanted to get close to me to get entree to my brother Wade, the investor. Seems she had this idea to start a five-star restaurant in Houston and she needed a backer with the intelligence to recognize a good idea and who had pockets deep enough to bankroll the operation during the year or so it would take to get it up and running successfully. And that was Wade."

"So she got involved with you and used you to wangle an invitation to meet him."

Jackson nodded. "The crazy thing was, it probably

never would have gone that far if I'd just been more
willing to bring her home to meet the family or at least
arranged for her to have dinner with Wade in the first
place. But I made it clear early on that I was through
standing in line for anyone's attention on the home
front, and then, when I was willing to, when I'd fallen
hard for her and *wanted* her to meet the family, my
life as a med student kept interfering. By the time my
schedule cleared enough to get home for a weekend,
six months had passed, and I'd decided to ask Amelia
to marry me, and where else was I going to do that but
at the ranch?" Restless now, Jackson pushed to his feet
and shoved a hand through his hair.

He moved to the window and stood there, staring
out at the quiet small town streets. Shrugging, Jackson turned back to face Lacey. Leaning one shoulder
against the pane, he continued, "So we went out there,
and she met Wade, and next thing I know she's getting
him off to the side, telling him she had this idea she
knew he'd want to invest in. Fortunately," Jackson's
lips curved sardonically, "Wade saw what was going
on right away and he turned her down."

Lacey's green eyes softened with compassion. "Did
you confront her?"

With an engagement ring burning a hole in my
pocket, Jackson thought bitterly. With effort, he pushed
aside the humiliation he still felt about that—about how
easily he'd been made a fool of by a pretty and ambi-
tious woman. Aware Lacey was waiting to hear the
rest of the story, he finished recounting the details
grimly. "Not surprisingly, once the cat was out of the
bag, it didn't take Amelia long to admit Wade was the

McCabe she'd had her eye on all along, that if she'd been able to meet him, she never would have targeted me and arranged to bump into me at that party."

Lacey who had met all of the McCabe sons at his dad's bachelor party, looked shocked and upset. "Surely, after six months of dating, her feelings for you were genuine!"

Jackson only wished there had been real love there—at least at some point—it would have soothed his damaged ego. But there hadn't been. Not then, not ever. When Amelia had looked at him with love in her eyes it had been money and the possibility of success she had been seeing, not him. "She saw me as a means to an end," Jackson explained. "So I broke it off." He shrugged. "And haven't seen Amelia since."

Lacey bit her lower lip. "Any idea what happened to her?"

Jackson nodded. "She found a sugar daddy to bank-roll her, and now owns three of the most successful new five-star restaurants in the state."

Lacey made a face. "Ouch."

Jackson rolled his eyes. He returned to the desk and sat down, kitty-corner from Lacey, who'd taken a side chair adjacent to him. "It was a lesson, all right, one learned the hard way. But it did sink in," he told Lacey firmly. "Never again am I going to be used as a means to an end. If I ever get involved with a woman again, to the point I will even think about asking her to marry me, she's not going to want or need anything from me but my love."

"Whoa!" Jenna Lockhart said that evening when Lacey emerged from the dressing room of her shop.

"My thoughts exactly," Lacey drawled as she spun around slowly in front of the three-way mirror. She didn't even look like herself.

"Hon, you sizzle in that dress."

Lacey studied her reflection and decided it was true. Of the dozen or so dresses she'd tried on when Jackson had brought her here, the one she and Jenna had selected for her to borrow and wear to the luncheon was definitely the best.

Made out of incredibly delicate and clinging fire-engine-red silk chiffon, the capsleeved dress sported a draped, off-the-shoulder portrait neckline, a fitted bodice, and a sleek, straight skirt that nipped in at her waist and hugged her bottom and ended four inches above her knees.

Lacey hadn't had shoes for it, but Jenna'd spent the last few days searching and had finally found the perfect shoes to accessorize it— a pair of sexy evening sandals with four-inch heels, in the exact same shade of red. She'd also produced a pair of skin-toned stockings with a hint of glitter and a red choker and teardrop earrings that perfectly complemented the dress. With her hair all loose and tousled and waved wildly from being confined in a braid, Lacey looked like a magazine cover girl.

It was just too bad, she thought in disappointment, that she wasn't going to have a chance to really wear the dress. But with a two-hundred-dollar price tag there was no way she could justify purchasing it for herself. Not for a single dress she'd never have any place to wear. Not in Laramie, anyway. This dress was big-city chic.

"Jenna's right. You do look incredible," Trey Johnston, the photographer said.

"So incredible I bet I'll up orders from my portfolio of designs immediately, once I start running the ad in next Saturday's editions of the Dallas and Houston newspapers," Jenna predicted, smiling, as she helped prepare for the photo shoot.

"How is business going?" Lacey asked as she pivoted slowly to let Jenna study the mix of dress, shoes, stockings and jewelry with a critical eye.

Jenna shrugged. "I've got plenty of women all over the state calling to make appointments to have a dress created especially for them, but I still haven't been able to interest a department store in carrying any of my designs. And until I get major exposure, well, it's just a dress here and there. There's no real fame or money in it." Jenna's discouragement was obvious.

"You're so talented. It's going to happen for you. One of these days soon, you'll be known as Texas's answer to Donna Karan."

"I hope so. But in the meantime let's pin this flower in your hair and let Trey photograph you under the lights."

For the next half hour, Lacey posed repeatedly. She'd never had any modeling experience, but Trey and Jenna made it easy for her. Finally they had what they needed, and Lacey headed back for the dressing room to change.

"What do you think Jackson's going to say when he sees you in it?" Jenna asked, as Lacey took off her shoes.

What she'd like him to do was let out a wolf whistle,

Lacey thought. But knowing Jackson—and his knack for always wearing exactly the right clothes and doing and saying the right thing himself—he was likely to be as unhappy with her attire as he was stunned. Which was, she admitted to herself, sort of the point of the whole thing.

"I'm hoping he'll beg me to switch it for my navy blue dress, pronto, before I embarrass us both. You know what he said the other evening when he brought me over here and insisted I get a proper dress for the luncheon—the women he goes out with have to dress as stylishly as he does." Lacey grinned impishly as she swept a hand down her body. "This hot little red number would be a gaff of the highest order for a day-time luncheon with the Pink Ladies."

Jenna chuckled. "I'd give anything to see the look on his face when you show up in it."

Lacey grinned. "I'll tell you all about it. Promise."

Lacey had no plans to see Jackson that evening, but somehow it didn't surprise her to find his Porsche parked out in front of Jenna Lockhart's shop when she emerged from the photo shoot. Jackson was perched on the hood of his car, ankles crossed in front of him, one hand—bearing a paper cup of something icy—propped on his thigh. He was dressed in faded blue jeans, alligator boots and a khaki Ralph Lauren work shirt. A Stetson—the exact same hue of his shirt—shadowed his brow.

As she approached, he tipped his hat back with one finger. "So what's in the garment bag?" He nodded at the zippered bag she'd slung across her arm.

Trying not to show how glad she was to see him, or let on just how bleak an evening without Jackson had seemed to her, Lacey sauntered closer. "My dress for the luncheon."

Jackson narrowed his eyes at her. "You didn't change your mind about wearing it, did you?"

Lacey shook her head. "No." In fact, considering how great she looked in the dress, she wouldn't miss seeing the expression on his face for the world.

Jackson breathed a sigh of relief. "In that case, since I never did see it the other night, mind if I take a peek?" He reached for the zipper.

Lacey put her hand over his. Ignoring the warmth and the strength, she pushed it away deliberately. "Not until tomorrow, cowboy."

He took a long sip of his icy drink. "Making me wait, huh?"

Lacey nodded. "You bet."

Jackson tilted the paper cup toward her and offered her a sip of his drink. "I still can't believe you actually bought a new dress just for me."

Lacey steadied the straw with her hand as she took a long, thirsty sip.

"Take as much as you want," he encouraged.

"Thanks. That lemonade hit the spot. And actually, I didn't buy the dress. It's on loan."

Jackson patted a place next to him, indicating she should perch there, too. Unable to think of a reason why she shouldn't, Lacey sat down next to Jackson, her blue-jeans-clad thigh nudging his in the process.

"I didn't know Jenna Lockhart loaned out her creations," Jackson continued.

Damn but he was perceptive. Wasn't there anything that got by him? Lacey wondered. Lacey smiled. "Normally she doesn't. But in this case she thinks it'll be good advertising for everyone to see me in the dress she designed, so she agreed to waive any purchase fee as long as I give it back as soon as I'm finished with it, and in return she took a few publicity photos of the dress tonight."

Jackson's glance roved the loose, tousled waves of her honey-blond hair, skipped briefly to her mouth and breasts before returning to her eyes. "It's that great on you, huh?"

Given the opportunity to tease him, Lacey couldn't resist. "Guaranteed, it'll take your breath away."

Jackson's sexy grin widened. Mischief sparkled in his eyes. "Now you're really making me curious," he drawled, offering her another sip of his lemonade.

Lacey just smiled and drank deeply from the straw.

"So how did Seth's interview go?" Jackson asked. When she'd finished drinking, he put the condensation-covered cup back on his thigh.

Lacey's spirits fell just a tad. Was that why he'd really sought her out? To check up on the professional competition? Maintaining an easygoing smile she couldn't begin to feel, she turned away and studied the family down the street. Mother, father and three children were all lining up for ice cream cones. "Smashingly. They all loved him."

Lacey thought she saw disappointment flash briefly in Jackson's sea-blue eyes but it was gone as quickly as it had appeared.

"That's good." Jackson nodded approvingly and

continued in a low, smooth voice. "The hospital needs a man like him." He stopped to take another sip of lemonade and turned to watch the family eating ice cream, too. Finally, he turned back to her. "When will you hear if he's going to accept the position or not?"

"He said by next Monday, if not sooner. He's got a few more interviews lined up, in other Texas cities. He'll talk to everyone before making a decision."

Jackson switched his paper cup to the other hand and rubbed at a damp spot on his jeans. "And if he turns it down...?"

"Not to worry." Lacey blew out a gusty breath and tried not to be aware of just how recently Jackson had showered and how smooth his jaw looked. "I'll just keep going down the list of possible candidates."

In other words, he was off the hook, Lacey thought. She was seriously looking to put someone else in the position so he could leave Laramie and not look back. That ought to make him feel good; yet—it didn't seem to.

"Why the sad look?" Lacey asked. He'd already said he didn't want the job.

Jackson pressed his lips together. "It just hit me." He looked at her and didn't turn his eyes away. "I'll miss seeing you."

A soft, shimmery feeling filled Lacey's middle. Trying not to let herself get too caught up in the moment, Lacey retorted softly, "We don't have to stop seeing each other."

Jackson continued to look at her a long moment, then turned back to the damp spot on his jeans. He went back to rubbing, more aggressively now. "We don't." He spoke as if he didn't quite believe that.

There'd been a time when Lacey hadn't either. Now—she felt different. Wanting to comfort him Lacey covered his hand with hers. "We could be friends, you know," she suggested gently. It might even make up for the fact she had come after him with an unwelcome agenda just the way Amelia had, thereby realizing one of his worst nightmares and causing him to come after her in the same fashion in return.

Jackson shook his head and drained the rest of his drink. He got up, tossed the cup in the nearest trash can, then strode back to her side. He sat down next to her once again. "I don't know if I could be just friends with you, Lacey," he said seriously, "after those kisses we shared."

Lacey wasn't at all sure of that, either, but the only alternative was to take the passion further, and with him leaving Laramie in a few short weeks, well, even he could see why that wasn't wise. Yet she didn't want to lose the camaraderie, the ability to confide in each other and count on each other—professionally and personally—that they'd forged, either. "Sure you could," she advised easily. "Just put the passion on the back burner."

Jackson took off his hat, set it half on his thigh, half on hers. He combed his fingers through his hair.

"Easier said than done."

"No, it's not," Lacey picked up her garment bag and his hat. She waited until he slung the Stetson back on his head, then took his hand in hers and led him determinedly down the street, toward her mom's bakery. "And I'll prove it to you."

"I guess this makes it official," Jackson drawled humorously a scant ten minutes later as Lacey removed the dough from the bakery refrigerator. "There is absolutely no end to your talents." He watched her measure out enough dough for a half-dozen doughnuts. "Did your Mom teach you how to do this?"

Lacey shook her head. "I worked part-time in a bakery all through high school and college. I got up and made doughnuts for three hours every morning before school." Lacey adjusted the temperature on the fryer. "I got so good at it I could practically do it in my sleep. In fact," Lacey laughed softly, recollecting, "there were probably some mornings when I did do it in my sleep." Stepping behind him, she reached her arms around him and put her hands over his, demonstrating deftly as she instructed. "Roll the dough out evenly like this. We want it to be about half an inch thick."

Jackson did his best not to be distracted by the fragrant floral scent of her hair and skin. "Then what?"

Lacey smiled. "Then we cut it into circles using a cutter and pile the doughnut holes over here to fry up, too."

For the next several minutes the two of them labored in silence. Not surprisingly, she was much better at lifting the dough off the floured board without distorting the shape than he was. "Is this the first time for you in the kitchen?"

Jackson was embarrassed by his clumsiness. There

were so few things he couldn't do well. Who knew this would be one of them? "Shows, huh?"

"A little." Carefully Lacey checked the temperature on the fryer, then slid the dough in. "What kind of part-time jobs did you hold as a kid?" she asked as the doughnuts puffed up as if by magic in the sizzling oil. "Or did you?"

Relieved to be done assisting, Jackson lounged against the counter and folded his arms in front of him. It surprised him how much he enjoyed just being with her like this. And it disturbed him to think that if he moved to Fort Worth as planned, and she stayed here in Laramie as planned, that evenings spent together like this would no longer be the norm, no matter how good or strong their friendship got to be.

Aware she was waiting for his answer, Jackson smiled. "I had jobs. My brothers and I all did. Travis worked on cattle ranches, Shane worked with horses, Wade worked as a runner for a law firm that specialized in real estate, and I worked for the hospital lab."

Lacey turned the doughnuts over. "So you knew even then you wanted to be a doc."

Jackson nodded. "I got interested, way back, just listening to my dad talk about some of his cases and watching him work with patients." He paused to rub a bit of flour from her nose. "What about you? When did you know?"

Still keeping an eye on the sizzling doughnuts, Lacey slipped onto a nearby stool. "My dad had a massive heart attack when I was eight. My mother and I were both there when it happened, but neither of us knew CPR, and he died before the ambulance could get there." Lacey took a deep breath as Jackson closed the distance between them and slipped a comforting arm about her shoulders. "They said the damage was so severe that even if we had administered CPR it's unlikely he would have lived."

"I'm sorry." Jackson tightened his grip on her.

Face pale, she accepted his expression of sympathy with a nod and turned her head into his chest as her fingers came up to pleat his shirt. "Afterward, I wanted to—I needed to—know more about what had happened and why, and what, if anything could have been done to prevent it. And the more I read, the more interested I got. So the summer I was fourteen, I got on as a candy striper at the local hospital, and as they say, the rest was history. I was hooked and stayed on track ever since." She glanced over at the doughnuts, which Jackson noted had turned a lovely golden brown. Lacey hopped off the stool. "They're done." She slid the perfectly cooked pastries out of the fryer and laid them gently on paper towels to drain. "Now for the pièce de résistance." She sprinkled them with cinnamon sugar, then gently turned them with a pair of tongs and sprinkled the other side.

Jackson's mouth watered as he watched her work. "I don't think I've ever had doughnuts this fresh," Jackson said.

"Then you are in for a real treat," Lacey promised cheerfully as she brought out a pitcher of milk from the fridge. She poured two tall glasses of milk, then scooped up a doughnut hole, still warm and covered with cinnamon sugar, popped it into his mouth, then popped one in hers. Jackson and Lacey groaned in unison as the soft, yeasty confection melted on their tongues. "Mmm. This is so good," he said, reaching for another.

"Isn't it?" Lacey grinned. For the next couple minutes they gorged themselves and washed down their treat with big gulps of milk. "Now was this worth the effort or not?" Lacey asked.

"Definitely worth it," Jackson said. "If only to see—" he reached up and touched her face again "—this." He rubbed the pad of his thumb across the milk mustache on her upper lip. Lacey's lips parted. Her whole body softened and leaned into his. The next thing Jackson knew he had her in his arms and he was kissing her. Hotly. Rapaciously. And she had wreathed her arms around his neck and moved all the way into his arms and was kissing him back just as hotly and just as rapaciously. And it was then—the very second he had tugged her even closer yet, so they were touching from shoulders to knees—that they heard footsteps on the stairs and a soft giggle.

Reluctantly Jackson lifted his head. He and Lacey drew apart. In tandem, they looked up and saw not just Lacey's mother, but her mother's two houseguests, too. Molly Weatherby grinned with a five-year-old's exuberance, aimed her finger at Lacey and Jackson and said, "Busted!"

Chapter 8

"Molly Weatherby is feeling a lot better now, isn't she?" Jackson remarked long minutes later, when he and Lacey were alone again.

"She says she is. And according to her mom and my mother she's eating a little better," Lacey confirmed. She bit into her lower lip. "But she's still looking pretty peaked and that worries me."

Jackson's blue eyes darkened compassionately as talk turned to Lacey's five-year-old patient. "For all her clowning around, you don't think Molly's completely shaken whatever it was that was making her sick, do you?"

Glad to confide her suspicions in another physician, Lacey candidly confirmed this was so. "If it were just stomach flu, I'd expect her to have a little more color in her face by now."

"What about her other symptoms and test results?" Jackson asked, looking equally concerned.

"They were all negative." Lacey shrugged. "I hope I'm overreacting here."

"But your gut tells you you're not."

"Right." Lacey paused. "Which is why I'm so relieved we were able to talk Patricia into staying in town a few more days. This way I can keep an eye on Molly a little longer—until she is feeling one-hundred percent—and give her a clean bill of health before she leaves. That is, if she and her mom leave Laramie at all."

Jackson looked intrigued. "You think they might stay?"

"I don't know." Lacey wrapped up the extra doughnuts for Jackson to take home with him. "Patricia and Molly both seem to like Laramie a lot and find it quite livable." She just wished Jackson did, too.

Jackson grinned, his mind clearly on other things as he rubbed a hand across his jaw. "They were also quite amused to catch us in a clinch."

Lacey blushed at his quip, knowing it was all too true. The two of them had not only raised some eyebrows—they'd raised some hopes as well. Molly hadn't been able to stop babbling about how romantic it was to find them kissing like that, and Patricia and Isabel had both concurred—after getting over their initial surprise—that Lacey and Jackson made a very cute couple indeed.

"You can stop blushing now," Jackson teased as Lacey turned away and continuing her clean-up operation, spritzed disinfectant cleaner over the stainless steel countertops in the bakery kitchen. "Kissing someone you're attracted to is a very normal activity. Neither of us has anything to be embarrassed about."

"I know that," Lacey murmured dryly. "It's just—" Lacey paused and shook her head self-consciously as Jackson helped her wipe down the counters with paper toweling "—it's not every day my mother catches me necking in her bakery."

Finished, Jackson took the soggy paper towel from her hand and tossed it into the trash. He grinned and turned his head toward her. "You don't sneak in and cook up a batch of doughnuts often, huh?"

"Not lately, and never with a beau."

A smile spread across his ruggedly handsome features as he propped himself up against one of the walls. His eyes held hers. "Is that what I am to you—a beau?"

Lacey switched off the overhead light, so all that remained was the soft light over the stove. She swung her gaze up to his. She had trouble catching her breath. "It felt like it tonight."

"To me, too."

She swallowed hard and stepped toward him.

"So what are we going to do about it, Lacey?" Jackson asked, very low.

Lacey had only to look into his eyes to know what he wanted to do. She shrugged and tore her gaze from the strong column of his neck. "What is there to do? You're leaving—"

Jackson curved an arm about her waist and hauled her close. His eyes connected with hers and held for a long, breath-stealing moment. "Not for three and a half more weeks," he reminded in a low, sexy voice that brooked no denial. His lips brushed the top of her head and nuzzled in the softness of her hair. He pulled her closer so they were touching everywhere.

The prospect of making love with Jackson made her heart beat even harder. Lacey resisted the urge to lean her head against the solidness of his shoulder. It would be so easy to give in to him, she thought. Too easy. Splaying the flat of her hand across his chest, she wedged a few very important inches between them and tried not to think how much she liked the tantalizing scent of his aftershave.

Feeling her cheeks grow ever warmer, she tilted her face up to his. "I told you how I felt about having flings. I'm just not in the market for one."

His sea-blue eyes were steady as they probed hers. "I'm not in the market for just a fling with you, Lacey." He leaned forward and placed another light kiss on her neck, then traced the outline of her lower lip with his thumb. "A fling would never be enough."

Lacey's breath hitched in her chest. "What are you saying?" she demanded. She couldn't afford to misunderstand or misinterpret this, and if she didn't know better, she'd think— by the way he was behaving—that he was desperately in love with her.

Jackson shrugged and determinedly held her gaze. "I'm saying," he said bluntly, "that maybe we should forget about how and why this all started and see about having a real relationship."

Lacey's hopes fell just as swiftly as they had risen. She'd wanted him to talk about his feelings, to tell her he was desperately in love with her. Instead, he was dwelling on specifics and the semantics of them, in an all-male, businesslike way. She exhaled a short little breath. "You mean a two-city, occasional, long-distance type thing," she said, unable to completely hide her disappointment.

He shook his head and took her lightly by the arms. "I mean a one-man, one-woman thing that exists whether we are both in the same city or not," he told her softly, then purposefully, "A one-man, one-woman thing that has us seeing each other as much as possible, and talking on the phone when we can't."

Lacey gulped. Finding it impossible to think clearly when he was holding her that way, she slipped out of his grasp. Turning her back to him, she waltzed around the kitchen restlessly. "You think that's what you want now," she said as she stared out the back door, to the neat-as-a-pin alley beyond. She was just as frustrated with their situation as he was. "But when you have time to think about it…" Her heart in her throat, Lacey swung around to face him and continued to try to keep herself—and Jackson—from getting hurt. "When your head and heart aren't still humming with the aftereffects of all that sugar—"

Jackson grinned, appreciating her feeble attempt at a joke. "And all those kisses."

"—we just consumed. You'll change your mind," Lacey vowed, staring fixedly at a point just beside his collar.

Jackson smiled and reached for his hat. But—to her disappointment—not for her. "No, I won't," he said softly and deliberately, showing himself to the door before she could take the matter in hand and do it for him. He settled his hat on his head. His sea-blue eyes gleamed with reckless lights. "And I'll prove it to you before the month is over."

"What happened to the dress from Lockharts?" Jackson asked the next day when he met her at her office shortly before noon. In deference to the luncheon they were about to attend in his honor, he was dressed in a beautifully tailored sand-colored suit that made the most of his tall, broad-shouldered frame and dark good looks. He looked very sexy and sophisticated in a decidedly urban way.

Nervously Lacey smoothed the skirt of her navy-blue dress. She knew the dress was attractive on her, if conservative and plain, but she couldn't help feeling a little frumpy next to him.

Unable to look into his sea-blue eyes without re-membering how bereft she'd felt the evening before, when he'd left without so much as even attempting to kiss her goodbye, she focused on the eclectic sable and sand design of his stylish necktie.

"I changed my mind." She nodded at the garment bag draped over the back of the sofa. "I'm taking it back."

Confused, Jackson ran a hand across his clean-shaven jaw. "Why?" he asked, stepping close enough to tease her senses with the invigorating fragrance of soap and aftershave and man. His lips curved into a coaxing smile. "I thought you said the dress you got on loan from Jenna was perfect for today."

Lacey flushed self-consciously, all too aware of the prank she had intended to play on him. "Well, it's not," she said stiffly, flushing all the more, telling herself she was glad she had come to her senses.

"Uh-huh." Jackson looked her up and down, came swiftly to a conclusion and did a sharp about-face. Realizing what he was about to do, Lacey tried to cut him off at the pass by darting in front of him and putting out an arm to bar his way. She hadn't expected him to be so nosy. To protest, maybe, but this? "Jackson— don't!"

Too late, he had already pushed past her to the sofa. Grabbing the garment bag and holding it out of reach, he swiftly pulled down the zipper and caught an eyeful of fire-engine-red silk chiffon.

The smile on his face was sexy and immediate.

"Whoa!" He swung around to face her, a mixture of pleasure and anticipation in his sea-blue eyes.

Lacey put a hand over her face. "I know," she moaned out loud, thinking she knew exactly what he was thinking. That was one incredibly sexy evening dress. And she had picked it out and expressly gone to one heck of a lot of trouble, especially for him. Jackson grinned, appreciating the bad girl in her all the more. "You were really going to wear this?" He gazed at her in wide-eyed pleasure, and Lacey could see him mentally making love to her, right where he stood. She flushed self-consciously and tried not to acknowledge just how much she was beginning to actually want him to do just that.

Figuring she might as well confess—he was bound to figure out what she'd had planned anyway—she swallowed hard and said, in the most low-key manner possible. "Obviously, it was a prank. And a very juvenile one at that. I was going to put it on and then have you talk me into wearing what I originally planned to wear anyway." She swept her hand down her body, demonstrating. "My good-for-any-occasion navy blue dress."

Jackson fingered the thin red silk and made a low, growly man-on-the-prowl sound in the back of his throat. "I gotta tell you, Lacey. If it comes down to a choice between this and the navy blue, fetching as it is—" He gave her and her navy blue dress a long sexy once-over, then waggled his eyebrows at her suggestively. "I think I like this."

Lacey grinned ruefully. She just bet he did. But the dress had to go back to Jenna's dress shop. She had already determined it was too extravagant a purchase when she had nowhere to wear it and no one to wear it for. And like it or not, with Jackson still planning to leave Laramie at month's end, that was not going to change.

Stepping forward, she grabbed the back of his hand, plucked his caressing fingers unceremoniously from the incredibly erotic red fabric and rezipped the garment bag. "This is most definitely not appropriate for the luncheon," she told him sternly, thinking of his highly enthusiastic reaction to just seeing the sexy dress on a hanger! Thank goodness she'd come to her senses in time and decided not to get him all riled up, modeling it for him!

Jackson shrugged and continued to eye her in a very predatory, very male way. "Maybe it's not appropriate for today." He grinned lazily and murmured seductively in her ear, "But I can think of any number of occasions where it'd be a great dress to wear."

Her skin tingling from the heat of his breath on her skin, Lacey turned away from the desire she saw in his eyes. Being that close to him had put all her senses in overdrive! "Sorry, Jackson, the dress is going back to Lockhart's today." There was too much heat between them as it was. All she had to do was be near him and her breasts ached, her tummy fluttered, her thighs went fluid and her knees went weak. No, she was much too easy prey where a seduction was concerned to tempt the fates that way.

Her decision made, Lacey expected him to protest—to tell her she was sexy and uninhibited enough to wear the dress anywhere, any time she chose.

But instead Jackson merely regarded her a long, thoughtful moment, then nodded—as if in total agreement—and joined her at the door. "The Pink Ladies are waiting." He held out his arm. "Shall we go?"

To Lacey's chagrin, the gossip started even before they entered the banquet room. And it continued throughout the stellar meal. Every time she turned around, she caught wind of yet another whisper.

"I didn't believe it when I heard—but they really are a couple!"

"Jackson McCabe, dating a woman more than once or twice?"

"As I live and breathe!"

"I heard they've been together every night since Jackson's been in town and Lacey jumped out of that cake at his father's bachelor party!"

A chorus of soft, feminine laughter ensued. "Guess she caught his eye, but good!"

Another wistful sigh. "If only I'd thought of that— think he would be chasing me?"

"I think we're out of luck, girls. We have to face it. He only has eyes for her."

Not surprisingly, Jackson did not look at all displeased with the turn of events.

"We're the talk of the luncheon," Jackson leaned over and whispered in Lacey's ear as dessert of peach cobbler and cinnamon ice cream was served.

"Don't I know it," Lacey whispered back, still flushing from the latest accidentally overheard conversation. She shook her head. "The way things are going, I'm never going to be able to live this down, even after you leave."

But their appearance together had served its purpose, Lacey thought, unsure whether to be elated or depressed. As far as all the eligible ladies in the room were concerned, Jackson was officially off the market, because of her. As long as he kept seeing her while he was in town, he wouldn't be fielding—or more likely, ducking—tons of phone calls and invitations every day.

Jackson smiled at her sexily. "Who says you're going to want to live it down?"

Who indeed?

As they were leaving, Margaret came up to them. She didn't look at all nonplussed that her plan to embarrass Jackson or at least put him in a very difficult spot had failed miserably. "Jackson, could I have a word with you?" she asked politely.

To Lacey's surprise, Jackson kept his arm around

Lacey's waist and looked at Margaret with none of his former animosity. "Sure, Margaret," he retorted easily.

Thinking privacy was in order, Lacey started to extricate herself from Jackson's light, staying grip. There were times when three was a crowd. This was definitely one of them. "I'll leave you two alone." She started to extricate herself from Jackson's light staying grip, only to find he wasn't about to let her go. Nor was Margaret.

"No. You come too, Lacey." Margaret guided them into a private corner of the adjacent serving room. As soon as they were out of earshot of the others, Margaret looked at Jackson earnestly. "You were great to come today," she said as a guilty flush filled her cheeks. Sighing, she touched a hand to her bouffant auburn hair. "In fact, you were so great, I'm embarrassed. I realize it's time you and I let bygones be bygones and called a truce. We're not kids anymore."

Jackson studied her curiously. "You're sincere," he said, after a moment.

"Very." Margaret worried the buttons on the front of her tailored yellow jacket. "I'm hoping you'll meet me halfway."

"And if I don't?" Jackson asked with sudden suspicion. "What then?"

Dismayed to find him throwing a monkey wrench into the conversation when things had been going so well, Lacey elbowed him. "Jackson, for heaven's sake!"

Jackson refused to look at Lacey or to back down from the stand he had taken. Keeping his eyes firmly on Margaret's flushed face, he commanded gruffly, "Let her answer, Lacey." He paused. "What if I don't

Margaret? What if I return to our old prank-playing ways and one upmanship and did something else to get even with you for this? Then what? Would you still want to quit or would you want to get right back into it, and once again 'surprise' me in some way or another the next time I come back to Laramie?"

Margaret hesitated. She seemed to know a lot was riding on her answer, but her reply was firm as she looked at Jackson, her eyes full of regret. "Then I still quit," she said quietly, at last showing Jackson the civility and respect she'd long shown everyone else in the community.

Margaret shook her head ruefully, once again looking like one of the movers and shakers in the community instead of the overly competitive high school kid she had been. "We're too old for this, Jackson. Besides, it's time to let you know how much I do respect you. And really owe you." She smiled at him warmly. "If not for you, and the constant competition between us, I never would have known how much I could accomplish in my own life."

Abruptly Jackson grinned, too. "It goes both ways, Margaret."

They regarded each other peacefully. Margaret took his hand in hers and clasped it warmly. "I'm glad you feel so, too."

Jackson not only took her hand, he encased her in a hug—the warm, spontaneous, genuine kind true Texans gave their friends. When he and Margaret broke apart, it was official.

"Wow," Lacey murmured long moments later, after she and Jackson had said goodbye to the rest of the

Pink Ladies at the luncheon. Walking in lock step, she and Jackson headed back down the corridor, toward the wing of the hospital complex where all the doctors offices were. "An end to the truce."

Jackson grinned and rubbed his jaw, still looking a little shocked, but immensely pleased at the turnabout. "See?" he teased. "Miracles happen every day."

Achingly aware she didn't want their time together to end, Lacey replied dryly, "Yes, I know." She made a sharp right into her private office via the back door to her office suite.

"And I've got another one in mind," Jackson said, following and shutting the door behind him.

Lacey glanced at her watch. Aware she only had a few minutes before she was scheduled to start seeing patients, she asked, "What do you mean?" Lacey disappeared into the adjacent bath. Leaving the door slightly ajar, she slipped out of her dress and changed into the T-shirt, scrubs and sneakers she routinely wore for rounds.

"I talked to my dad," Jackson said from the other side of the door. "And got him to do a favor for us."

For us. Lacey liked the sound of that, even though she knew she shouldn't. Whipping her hair up into a ponytail, she came out to join him.

Jackson watched her put her navy blue dress on a hanger. "He's agreed to cover for you, starting tomorrow morning, so you and I can drive to Fort Worth." He strode forward gallantly to help her slip on her white lab coat. "I want to show you where I'm going to be working next month, Lacey," he said softly, assisting again as she straightened her collar and looped her stethoscope around her neck. "I want to show you where I'm going to be living."

Lacey froze, not sure whether that was a good idea or not. As much as she wanted to see where he was going to be living, she didn't want the reminder he was leaving. It was just too painful.

Jackson seemed to know that and wanted to get around it. He held up his hand in silencing fashion. "Please." Jackson regarded her earnestly. "Say you'll take the day off and go with me."

"So what do you think?" Jackson asked from the balcony of the high-rise condominium, overlooking downtown Fort Worth.

"It's beautiful," Lacey said, meaning it. The luxurious condominium was incredibly elegant inside and out, with top-of-the-line everything. And the spacious balcony with its high stone walls provided both privacy and a place to enjoy the great outdoors. She could imagine relaxing out here after a long day.

Jackson's pleased expression said he agreed wholeheartedly with her assessment. He studied the city spread out across the Texas plains like a glistening jewel. Quiet moments later, he pivoted back to her, watching her expression closely. "Do you like this better than the two-story town house we saw earlier?"

Lacey shrugged, uncomfortably aware she wasn't the one who was going to be living here. Only Jackson was. And that bothered her more than she wanted to admit. "It's hard to say. They're both very elegant." And expensive. If Jackson lived here, there would be no questioning his success.

Jackson frowned and went back to reading the brochures in hand with single-minded determination. "The other place had a garden adjacent to the private patio. This doesn't."

Lacey tried not to fidget. "You could put plants up here, too," she said casually. "There's plenty of room."

"True." Jackson smiled and looked around as if imagining just that.

"And—" Lacey tried to pretend for just a minute that this kind of thing mattered to her "—here you have a magnificent view. Plus it's a little closer to the hospitals and your group practice's office."

Jackson put the brochures in the pocket of his mocha ultrasuede sport coat. He closed the distance between them. "So you'd be happy with either."

She'd be happy, Lacey thought, if she could just find a way to make him forget all this—the accoutrements of success—and just stay in Laramie. With her. But that wasn't going to happen. He'd made that very clear to her from the start. And she had to deal with it. And deal with him, honestly.

When he took her in his arms, Lacey splayed her hands across his chest. "It's all about what makes you happy, Jackson," Lacey said, looking up at him. Beneath her fingertips, his heart took on a slow, heavy beat. Her knees got weak. Lacey swallowed and forced herself to go on, as if she really were happy and wanted all this for him, too. "After all, this is going to be your life, not mine," she told him gently.

Jackson sifted his fingers through her hair. He dragged a thumb lovingly across the curve of her cheek. "It could be yours, too," he pointed out softly.

Lacey tried like hell not to get lost in the mesmerizing blue of his eyes, but it proved an impossible task.
"What do you mean?" she asked hoarsely, unable to
tear her gaze away.

Jackson smiled as he dropped the pad of his thumb
and traced the curving, bow shape of her lips. "When
you visit me here, for starters."

Lacey leaned back slightly in the warm snug cradle
of his arms, putting space between her breasts and his
chest and wishing her mind weren't filled with wistful—or was it hopeful—thoughts of making love to
him. She sighed softly, aware all her dreams seemed
both very close to happening and equally far away.
"You really think that's going to happen?" She looked
deep into his eyes and just couldn't imagine it.

"I know it will," Jackson told her confidently. He
sifted his hands through her hair. And there in the
warm summer sunshine, beneath the beautiful blue
Texas sky, he took her face in his and kissed her long
and hard and deep, until her middle fluttered weight-
lessly and the rest of her was every bit as boneless as
her knees. When at last he released her, Lacey wasn't
the only one who was trembling. And aching for more.
"Ready to go to the hotel?" he asked her hoarsely.

Fighting a curious roller coaster of unbearable tension and thrilling anticipation, Lacey nodded.

The bellhop carried their bags into the luxurious
two-bedroom suite and set them down, along with a
beribboned gift box that had been held for them at the
front desk. Jackson tipped him. The door shut after
him. For a moment Jackson turned back to Lacey and

for a moment just stood there, savoring the sight of her. They'd been on the go for hours now, driving into the city at the crack of dawn, checking out the office where he would soon be hanging his shingle and touring the large, state-of-the-art hospitals where he'd be on staff. They'd looked at seven possible places for him to live, and of those, had finally narrowed it down to two. Through it all, Lacey had looked fresh and pretty in a sort of laid-back, down-home, Texas way. But now that evening was approaching and they were finally checked into the hotel where they'd be staying, she looked pale and upset and fidgety.

Figuring he needed to put her mind at ease and let her know they wouldn't be doing anything in either bedroom she didn't cheerfully volunteer to do, he sauntered closer. Gave her a reassuring smile. "You look like you're going to the guillotine," he teased gently, hoping a little humor would lighten the sudden tension between them.

"I can't help it." Lacey took a deep breath and looked around at her surroundings as if she was in a jail cell, not the finest hotel in all of Fort Worth, Texas. "I'm sorry, Jackson," she stammered. The flush in her cheeks deepened self-consciously. "I'm not going to be comfortable here."

If she needed a lock and key between them, so be it. Jackson shrugged and tried not to feel disappointed she didn't trust him more than that. "If you'd rather I call down and try and get separate rooms for us—" he volunteered, letting her know it was no big deal.

"It's not that." Lacey flushed all the more. Cupping her elbows in her hands, she began to pace back and forth, the heels of her bold blue boots digging into the thick carpet. She strode to the windows and looked out. "It's the price."

"And I told you," he repeated with all the patience he could muster, "with what I am going to be making, starting next month, I can afford to splurge once in a while." And there was no one he'd rather pamper this way than Lacey.

But clearly, he thought, studying the distressed expression on her lovely face, she did not see it that way. Determined to understand her unprecedented reaction, no matter how long it took, he crossed to her side and stood, one shoulder propped against the pane. Reaching up, he tucked a stray lock of hair behind her ear. "But that's not the issue, is it?" he prodded gently, realizing there had to be something more going on here. Something important.

"No." Lacey released a tremulous sigh as she stared up into his eyes. "It isn't."

"You want to tell me what's behind your frugality then?" Jackson pressed, still marveling that he could care as much about one woman as he cared about Lacey. There hadn't been a moment since he'd met her that he hadn't thought about her, or been grateful for her presence in his life. And that was the case even when she was being her most maddening, like now. "'Cause your mother isn't that way," Jackson continued, still studying her upturned face. "In fact, as I recall, she was the one urging you the other night to kick up your heels and pamper yourself a little more."

Lacey turned away from him and began to pace once again. "It's complicated."

Jackson caught the edge in her voice. Obviously this went a lot deeper than he had suspected. "Most feelings about money are," he told her gently, really wanting to understand her feelings on this issue and every other.

He closed the distance between them swiftly, took her hand in his and guided her over to the sofa. "Take mine, for instance," he said as he sat down and pulled her onto his lap. "We grew up knowing we would always have clothes to wear and food to eat and a roof over our heads, but when it went beyond that—when it came to taking vacations to Disneyland or getting the newest gizmo for our bicycles, my brothers and I were out of luck.

"Don't get me wrong," he said, putting up a hand before she could interrupt. "My parent's frugality helped put three of us through college—Shane refused to go—and buy the ranch that we all enjoy so much. But I was the third son and I spent my whole childhood wearing hand-me-downs from my two older brothers. Suffice it to say," Jackson continued dryly, thinking of some of the downright utilitarian outfits Travis picked out à la John Wayne and the flashy ones à la Maverick his brother Wade had favored even then, "our tastes in clothing were not the same." Jackson frowned. "I promised myself when the time came, when I was finally able to support myself, there'd be no more old clothes and no more putting off till tomorrow what could be enjoyed today.

"So," he smiled at Lacey and stroked her arm from shoulder to wrist, "unlike my folks, I am going to take vacations while I'm still young enough to enjoy them, and I am going to treat myself every now and then to something absolutely fantastic—like this hotel suite and a four-star dinner on the town with the woman I adore—when it's in my budget. And I'm telling you, Lacey," he said firmly, decisively, "this is in my budget. Otherwise, we wouldn't be doing it."

Lacey sighed and, turning slightly in his arms, met his eyes. "If only my father had thought that way," she told him sadly, "I might not be feeling the way I do now."

"What do you mean?" Jackson demanded gently.

Lacey splayed her hand across his chest, wishing he didn't look quite so much like a man to lean on in times of stress. She was used to dealing with things more or less alone, and there was a part of her—hidden deep inside—that still wanted to keep it that way.

But she also knew, if they were going to be the kind of man-woman friends—or more than friends that he seemed to want and she did, too—there were things he was going to have to understand about her. And bottom line, there was nothing more important than this.

Taking a deep, bolstering breath, Lacey gathered her courage and began to tell him how one of the darkest times of her life began. "My dad always wanted my mother and me to have the best. So while he was alive, we went everywhere and did everything." Warming to the kindness she saw in Jackson's eyes, Lacey leaned against the solidness of his chest. Her lips curved as she remembered fondly, "There were ski vacations at Christmas, summers in the mountains, lots of clothes and gifts and an incredibly beautiful home in a very nice section of Dallas. Not until he died did we find out how heavily he had mortgaged our lives and our futures." She shook her head, the old mixture of bitterness, bewilderment and betrayal gripping her heart. "Suffice it to say," she continued, "my mother and I lost everything—the house and the cars and the neighborhood I'd grown up in." The memories almost unbearable in their intensity, Lacey extricated herself from Jackson's arms, got up and began to pace the length of the suite. "It wasn't fashionable to be homeless then, but that's exactly what we were," she confided, her voice catching, her eyes filling with unshed tears as she spun around and forced herself to go on. "Less than a month after the funeral, we were out on the street, my mother scrambling to get a job."

"That's why you felt so sorry for Patricia and Molly Weatherby, isn't is?"

Lacey nodded and met Jackson's eyes. The kindness—the compassion—she saw in their depths gave her the strength to continue. "Because I'd been there." She knit her fingers together nervously. "My mother and I both had." Lacey's lips twisted bitterly. "And I'm telling you, Jackson, it's nowhere I ever want to go again."

He looked at her steadily. "You won't."

"Intellectually, I know that."

"But emotionally," he guessed as he ambled across the room to her side, "it's another matter."

Lacey nodded, the ache in her throat growing more pronounced, even as the ache in her heart eased. They stood facing each other in silence. Finally Jackson gripped her gently by the elbows. "Look, if you want, I'll go down and check us out of here and try to find us more modest accommodations. I don't mind."

Lacey shook her head. "But then you'd be paying double for tonight's lodgings."

"That's true." But he was willing to do it just the same if it would make her feel better.

Lacey shook her head firmly. "I can't let you do that."

Jackson studied her with growing curiosity, all the compassion he felt for her reflected in his eyes. "Then you'd be willing to stay here and try to enjoy yourself?"

Lacey's lips curved upward. "Just as long as you know I don't want to make a habit of such extravagance," she said bluntly, relieved he understood.

"Gotcha." Jackson grinned back. "But as long as we're going all out tonight, I've got something for you." He retrieved the gift box that had been waiting for them upon their arrival at the hotel. Lacey opened it, wondering what could be inside. When she found out, she was as shocked as she was delighted. "The dress from Lockhart's shop!" She had returned this last night, unworn. And had secretly regretted doing so ever since.

It seemed—up until this evening—that so much of her life had been about sacrifice and denial. And, like Jackson, she was beginning to grow tired of it all. She was beginning to grow tired of waiting for the perfect time to do anything and everything, because more and more it seemed like the perfect time would never come. At least not soon enough for her to enjoy it! And the thought of bypassing a passionate love affair in favor of something more permanent that might never come was even more disturbing. She didn't want to wake up one day and find out she had missed out on the one and only opportunity to discover real passion in her life. And that was, Lacey admitted to herself reluctantly, exactly what she was doing by continuing to hold Jackson at arm's length. She was betting that someone more suited to her would come along, when her heart and soul were telling her—almost continually—that this just wasn't so, that there was no better man for her than Jackson McCabe.

Aware she was as touched as she was pleased by the thoughtfulness of his gift to her, she turned to Jackson. "How'd you get this?" she asked, wondering how it was he knew so much about what she was thinking and feeling and secretly wishing for.

"I went over and bought it for you last night after you returned it," Jackson confessed.

Lacey'd thought he'd been pursuing her avidly before. She was beginning to see she hadn't experienced anything near his "full court press." But she felt she was about to.

His eyes danced, letting her know how much he enjoyed pampering her in every way possible. "Jenna told me you were born to wear it." Briefly he lifted her wrist to his lips and kissed the softness of her skin. Still regarding her sexily, he continued, "And I figured, as long as it had already been altered to fit you like a second skin, and you'd already agreed to wear it as advertisement for Jenna Lockhart's custom-design clothing shop, why not wear it here?"

They hadn't been kidding about the dress, Jackson realized a short while later. Just seeing Lacey in it made his blood heat and his mouth go dry. And with good cause. The fire-engine-red silk chiffon clung to her svelte body like a second skin, the low drape of the off-the-shoulder portait neckline revealing inches of creamy shoulders as well as the uppermost curves of her breasts. The fitted bodice hugged her ribs and waist like a lover's caress, and from there, fell straight, ending a tantalizing four or five inches above the knee. High heeled sandals in the same hue as her dress made the most of her sexy legs. Just looking at her, knowing she'd worn it just for him alone, made him feel happier and more optimistic than any man in his situation had a right. It made him feel like there might be some lovemaking in their future after all.

But not yet, Jackson determined as he released a slow, deliberate breath.

"We better get out of here," Jackson drawled, only half kidding as he guided her gallantly toward the door to their hotel suite, "while my gentlemanly intentions are still intact."

Lacey threw her head back, and her soft, feminine laughter floated up to his ears. He'd thought she looked good in scrubs and jeans, but both were nothing compared to this!

"That potent, hmm?" she teased.

"Oh, yeah, and then some," Jackson confirmed, feeling his lower body come alive in a way it never had before. He shook his head as another bolt of fire missiled into his groin. "When I saw it on a hanger," he murmured, groaning softly, "I had no idea…" None. That it would affect him this way.

"Neither did I." Lacey smiled, looking very, very pleased.

* * *

To Jackson and Lacey's mutual delight, their dinner was everything they could have wished for, the dancing that followed in the hotel's romantically lit piano bar even better. They returned to their suite to find a dozen red roses, a bucket of champagne on ice and a gift-wrapped box of chocolate truffles, all waiting for them.

Lacey looked at it all and shook her head. No one had done so much for her to make sure she had a wonderful evening since…well, she couldn't remember when. And that's what bothered her—the fact she could all too easily get used to this, only to have it go away.

Looking exceedingly handsome and sexy in a deftly tailored black tuxedo, Jackson dropped the room key on the table, crossed to her side and took her hand in his. "Too much?" he asked, lifting her fingers to his lips for a soft and tender kiss.

Lacey sighed contentedly. As much as she loved being spoiled this way, she didn't want to let herself get used to it, any more than she wanted him to think it was necessary. "Too much," she confirmed softly. Jackson was making the same mistake her father had. She didn't need presents. She didn't need luxury suites or the best of everything. She needed him. She needed time with him. She needed love and commitment and tenderness. And little more.

Wreathing his arms around her waist, Jackson guided her fully into his arms once again. She could feel him against her, so hard and so strong. Her heart thudded heavily at the knowledge he wanted her so much. And suddenly she knew what she hadn't before, that the two of them belonged together. Not just for a few days or weeks, but for all time. Tonight was not a fleeting moment she'd come to regret, but a beginning—a beginning she would treasure the rest of her life.

Framing her face with his hands, he forced her face up to his.

"Then what's it going to take to woo you?" Jackson demanded in a soft, urgent voice.

"Just this, Jackson," Lacey murmured softly, wreathing her arms about his neck, taking what he offered, what she had wanted and dreamed of her entire life. "Just this," she whispered, threading her hands through his hair.

Throwing her usual caution to the wind, she rose up on tiptoe, brought her lips up to his and kissed him with everything she felt, everything she wanted. And he kissed her back in the same all-encompassing way, his hand sliding around to find her breast, cupping gently as his kiss deepened, his tongue probing eagerly in the deep recesses of her mouth, bringing forth responses she didn't know she had in her, responses she wanted to feel again and again and again.

She could feel his erection pressing against her as they kissed—languidly at first, then with growing ardor. The strokes of his hands, his lips, his tongue became more insistent. Her breast swelled in his hand, the nipple hardening against his palm, and a tingle arrowed through her, sliding down to pool in the pit of her tummy, then lower still, to the most feminine part of her. Lacey melted against him helplessly. And still he kissed her, until her thighs went fluid and her knees weakened, until she was swaying against him, trembling from head to toe.

It felt so good to be wanted and touched. She wanted him to feel the same.

She thrust her tongue into his mouth, tentatively at first, then more boldly. Her hands stroked across his shoulders, then down to touch his hard-muscled chest through the starched cotton of his shirt.

His mouth fused with hers as if they were two integral parts of a whole, and he groaned as her palms slipped beneath his jacket and slid around his back, massaging the hard-muscled contours on either side of his spine. "We have got—" he declared huskily as he anchored an arm about her waist, lifted her off her feet and carried her to the nearest bed "—to get these clothes off!"

Lacey laughed. "Agreed." When he slowly lowered her feet to the floor, she stepped back, out of the circle of his arms. She wanted to feel all of him against all of her. But first she wanted to see all of him. Nevertheless, not sure where—how—to start, she remained motionless and mesmerized.

A seductive smile tugging at the corners of his lips, he stepped behind her. One gentle fist capturing and holding up the length of her hair, he kissed the back of her neck, then dropped a line of kisses down her bare skin, until he reached the hook at the top of her dress.

"This first," he declared, loosening it and drawing the zipper down. Cool air streamed over her heated skin as he drew the silk chiffon dress carefully down her arms, torso, waist, hips. Heart pounding, Lacey rested her weight on his arm and stepped out of it.

He let it drop to the floor beside them, then slowly pivoted her to face him. As his glance swept over her, appreciatively taking in her scantily clad form, there was no denying it. She'd never felt so beautiful or womanly in her life.

His hot blue eyes held her spellbound as he rapaciously surveyed the length of her, recklessly exploring every inch of her high-heeled sandals, strapless red silk bustier, garter belt, shimmery stockings and matching bikini panties.

"Sweetheart," he murmured playfully as he touched his lips to hers. "I had no idea you even had undies like this."

The truth was, Lacey thought as she kissed him back, she'd never even been able to imagine herself wearing something so sensual and blatantly seductive. Until he came into her life. This might have started out as a contest between them—a contest to see who could get whom to do what—but it had swiftly evolved into so much more. She wanted him—every bit as much as he wanted her—and that knowledge lent a reckless edge to an already dangerously uninhibited evening.

Kicking off one high-heeled sandal, then the other, Lacey put her arms about his neck. "Thank Jenna," Lacey whispered back, her lips curving wryly as she pressed all of her against all of him. "She's very big on accessorizing her clothing and sent them along with the dress—as the perfect accompaniment."

"And then some." Jackson let his gaze drift appreciatively over her again, taking in the soft swell of her breasts, the nip of her waist and the seductive flare of her hip. Unable to help himself, he gave a low wolf whistle. Lacey flushed with pleasure. Their gazes locked. And Jackson knew, just as he had when they'd entered the suite, that no matter what happened later, this was an evening they would both remember for the rest of their lives.

"So I take it this means you like it?" Vamping for him once again, Lacey swept her hand down her body and pivoted slowly.

Was it hot in here or what? Jackson wondered, loosening his tie.

"Oh, yeah." Jackson jerked off his tie with one hand, knowing that had been the understatement of the century, and began unbuttoning his shirt with the other. "I like it." So much he was afraid he wasn't going to be able to pace himself with the utter control and tender expertise Lacey deserved.

Maybe if she hadn't been so stunningly, heart-stoppingly gorgeous no matter what she was wearing, or had such a way of getting to him heart and soul, it would have been easier to make love to her, get her out of his system and move on. But now, seeing her this way, feeling about her the way he did, he no longer knew if it was possible to leave her for even a day. Which left him only one alternative, he decided firmly. To work harder to convince her to leave Laramie and come with him.

His emotions soaring, Jackson slid one arm around her waist, the other beneath her knees, and lowered her gently to the king-size bed. Her blond hair spread out across the pillows. It looked exactly as he thought it would in this situation, all soft and tousled and touchable. He sat down beside her on the edge of the bed, planting an arm on either side of her. "I want tonight to be special," he told her.

Her cheeks flushed and her eyes sparkled as she reached up to finish taking off his shirt. "So do I," she murmured. "And to that end, cowboy," she drawled, unbuckling his belt and starting on his fly. "Let's see if we can't make you a little more comfortable, too."

Minutes later they were lying naked beneath the crisp white sheets. Jackson drew Lacey into the cradle of his arms. Feeling intoxicated by her nearness, by the fact she was finally—finally—in his bed, he held her against him, closed his eyes and, just for a moment forcing himself to slow down, he touched his lips to the fragrant softness of her hair and skin. "I don't want to rush," he whispered.

Lacey looked up at him, her green eyes filled with longing as she kissed him back thoroughly. "I don't want to, either."

Determined to give her the kind of complete and thorough lovemaking she deserved, he kissed her the way he'd never kissed any woman. With passion so hot it sizzled. His tongue swept along hers, circled it and flicked across the edges of her teeth before dipping deep. Breathlessly she responded, the softness of her body giving new heat to his. His body trembling with the effort it was costing him to go slow enough to please her, he swept his hands down her body, deliberately discovering every silky curve, every sweet response. He kissed her until he heard her moan and felt her tremble, until their bodies melded in an instant of boneless pleasure.

Sliding down her body, he cupped the full weight

of her breasts with his hands, flicking the nipples with his thumbs before bending to pay homage with his lips and tongue. Quivering at the no-holds-barred intimacy of the caress, Lacey drew in a quick, urgent breath and dove her fingers through his hair. "Jackson—" Her voice caught. Pleasure swept through him, and trembling, she arched again.

Satisfaction flowing through him in effervescent waves, he kept up the sensual conquest, sliding back up to kiss her thoroughly, taking her mouth in a slow, hot, mating dance, palming her breasts and capturing the entire weight of the silky globes in his hand.

"Jackson," Lacey whispered, as she kissed him again. Fiercely this time. With a yearning that was not to be denied. She trembled, her nipples pressing urgently against his palms. She surged against him. Hot, excited color filled her cheeks. "I want—"

"I know," Jackson whispered back and, satisfaction—that he could make her feel this way—pouring through him, he rubbed his hands across her nipples again and again until she sucked in her breath and arched against him, sinuously, exultantly. "I know exactly what you want." He kissed her again, wanting their time together, this slow sensual possession of her, to never stop. "You want this." He rubbed his chest across her bared breasts, tantalizing her budding nipples with the silky mat of his chest hair and the hard muscles beneath. "And this."

Triumphing in the sexy floral scent of her, he slid his lips across the softness of her breasts, to the tautness of her abdomen. Reveling in the softness of her body, he kissed his way down her body, to the velvety honey-blond curls. She whimpered as he traced a hand down the silky length of her thighs and in between.

Not wanting to proceed any further until she was gloriously wet, gloriously ready, he kept up his tender explorations and kisses, loving her with his mouth and hands and tongue, not stopping until she moaned softly and surged against him, falling apart in his arms. Loving the strength of her response to him, he slid up to join her on the pillows, caught her in his arms, and held her until her shudders stopped.

"No fair," Lacey murmured breathlessly as Jackson rolled onto his back, taking her with him. She dropped her head and kissed his chest. "You let me race on ahead."

Jackson grinned as he toyed with her hair. "I'll catch up," he promised hoarsely, meaning it. The way he was feeling, it wouldn't take long at all.

"You certainly will," Lacey promised softly, slipping away from him.

Wanting him to lose control in the same way she just had, Lacey kissed her way down Jackson's chest, enjoying the hair-roughened texture and the feel of the muscle beneath. He'd driven her to distraction. Now she drove him to the brink, sending him into a frenzy of wanting as the last of her inhibitions melted away. She found him with her hands, touching and worshiping, taking her time, until his desire surged against her fingers, silky, warm and liquid. Then slid lower still, until his hands curled in her hair, holding her against him, and the sensation of her lips on him was more than he could bear.

Hands on her shoulders he groaned at the pleasure

she was giving him and brought her up to face him, then turned her, so she was once again beneath him. "Now?" Lacey whispered softly, linking her arms around his neck.

"Now," Jackson said, the throbbing hardness of his body telling her of his urgent need for her.

"Good," Lacey whispered back tantalizingly. She kissed him slowly, lingeringly, as her body surged up to meet his. There was no denying their passionate need of each other, no denying the feelings swirling around in her heart, or the intent look in his sea-blue eyes. "Because I want you, Jackson," she whispered against the steady, building pressure of his lips. "I want you so much."

Jackson positioned himself between her thighs, the sensation of his manhood surging against her almost more than she could bear. "We belong to each other now," he whispered, moving ever so slowly and deliberately up and in.

"Yes," Lacey whispered, just as ardently, as he surged forward and deepened his penetration even more with slow, certain strokes. "Oh, yes..." And he was right, she thought, as the dizzying passion filled her senses and he drove her slowly, irrevocably to the heights of pleasure. They did belong to each other. Now. And always. For the first time in her life she knew what it was to want to be with a man, heart and soul. Jackson was the embodiment of every romantic fantasy she had ever had. And she wasn't going to let him go, Lacey thought, as the world fell away and they plummeted together into the cascading pleasure. Not now. Not ever.

Chapter 9

Lacey and Jackson were just snuggling down to sleep shortly after midnight when the phone rang. "Who would be calling us at this hour?" Jackson asked.

Her body still humming with the aftereffects of their lovemaking, Lacey reached past him for the phone. "I don't know, but it must be important. Otherwise they'd never telephone this late."

"Lacey!" Isabel said, relieved after Lacey had said hello.

The sheet drawn loosely to his waist, Jackson leaned back against the pillows. "Who is it?" he mouthed.

"My mother," Lacey mouthed back, before turning her attention to the phone once again. "What's up, Mom?" she asked, knowing it must be very important or her mother never would have telephoned.

"Oh, honey, I hate to bother you," Isabel said anxiously. "Patricia and I both do. But it's Molly."

The mention of her five-year-old patient had Lacey sitting up abruptly. "What about Molly?" Lacey demanded, shoving the tousled hair from her face.

"She can't sleep and she's just so pale!"

"Did you take her temperature?"

"It's 99.3. Now, I know—" Isabel rushed on "—technically that's not a fever—at least not yet, but Patricia and I are a little worried just the same, since Molly was just discharged from the hospital yesterday morning."

Roughly thirty-six hours before, Lacey calculated quickly.

"It's possible of course we let her do too much today," Isabel continued worriedly. "Patricia and I took her to the park for a picnic supper after I closed up the bakery for the day and she had so much fun playing on the swings and the slide that she barely touched her dinner. Now she says her tummy is a little sore again. Of course, it could be all the physical activity, causing that—"

Then again, Lacey thought, it could be something much more serious, and knowing that, her next decision was easy to make. She swung her legs over the side of the bed. "Listen, Mom, Jackson and I are coming home right away."

"Honey, I didn't mean to interrupt your holiday. I just want to know what to do—"

"I know, Mom." Lacey reached over, took Jackson's hand and squeezed it. "But I'll feel better once I take a look at her. Besides, we were headed back to Laramie first thing in the morning, anyway. The driving will go faster this time of night."

* * *

"What are you thinking?" Jackson asked, as they hurriedly began to dress.

Lacey frowned as she hunted around for their shoes. "That this recovery of Molly's wasn't a recovery at all—but rather, a misleading lull before the storm."

Jackson shared both her concern and her frustration. "I know there was no tenderness in the right-lower abdomen." He began to review the case with Lacey as he gathered up their belongings. "And if Molly's appendix is in the correct place, hanging down from the cecum, she definitely would have had that symptom."

"But," Lacey continued, thinking out loud along with Jackson, "if Molly is one of the very rare people whose appendix is located against the posterior side of the cecum, and bound there by the three tinea coli instead of hanging down, then she wouldn't have any tenderness in her right-lower abdomen. Which means the reason her symptoms disappeared abruptly after two or three days was not because she'd had gastroenteritis that had run its course, but because her appendix had ruptured."

Jackson nodded, agreeing with Lacey's worst-case scenario. "And this in turn relieved Molly's pain and fever because the stretching of the appendix also ceased. So she had a few days of feeling okay—until an abcess began to form around the ruptured appendix—"

Lacey frowned thoughtfully. "Which would in turn explain why her pain and fever are returning now." And why they had to leave immediately.

By the time Lacey and Jackson reached Laramie,

two hours later, Molly's fever had spiked to 102. She had considerable pain and nausea. One look at her and Jackson and Lacey both knew that Molly was obviously toxic and quite ill.

Jackson scooped Molly up in his arms while Lacey called the hospital to alert the O.R. and call in an anesthesiologist. Jackson took Patricia aside and explained the need for exploratory surgery while Lacey reassured Molly everything was going to be okay. Then the five of them climbed into the car and headed for the hospital.

Patricia and Isabel rose nervously to their feet as Lacey and Jackson strode into the waiting area. "How is she?" Patricia demanded, her hand flying to her throat, as Lacey's mom looked on in concern, too.

"Molly came through her surgery with flying colors," Jackson told Molly's mother happily.

"Was the problem what you thought?" Isabel asked anxiously.

Jackson nodded, then went on to explain with quiet confidence, "Molly's appendix was tucked behind her cecum, instead of hanging down from the end of it, which is what made the diagnosis of her illness so difficult. By the time we got in there, her appendix had ruptured, but we were able to remove it and drain the abcess, so she should be feeling a lot better very soon."

Lacey concurred with a smile, then added, "And Molly should even be able to go home from the hospital in a day or two."

"That's wonderful." Patricia's eyes brimmed with

tears of relief as she thanked them both. "Can I see her?"

Jackson nodded. "Just as soon as she comes out of the recovery room."

"Meanwhile I'll make sure they've got her room ready upstairs." Lacey headed for the phone at the nurses' station.

By 5:00 a.m. Molly was resting comfortably in a private room in the pediatrics wing, her mother beside her. Isabel had gone home to get another hour or two of sleep before opening her bakery. Too wound up to sleep yet, Jackson and Lacey headed for the McCabe ranch. As they drove up, Lilah and John McCabe were throwing suitcases in their extended-cab pickup truck. "Where are you off to?" Jackson asked curiously.

"Medical conference in Houston," John said.

"We're giving a seminar on the pluses and pitfalls of rural medicine. We'll be back tomorrow morning." Lilah smiled at them both curiously. "What are you two doing back here?" She paused again to study the blush of color in their faces. "I thought you weren't coming back till late this afternoon."

"That was the plan," Jackson drawled, "then Molly Weatherby's appendix ruptured." Briefly they explained. His parents were as relieved as everyone else about the good outcome.

"I'm sorry your minivacation was cut short," John told Lacey sympathetically. "But you still have another day to enjoy yourselves so feel free to stay at the ranch in our absence."

"Yes, absolutely," Lilah added. "There's no reason for you to be sleeping in an on-call room at the hospital, Lacey, when we have so many empty bedrooms here." She turned to her son. "Jackson, fix up the guest room for Lacey."

"I was planning on it."

Lacey turned to face him in astonishment. He was taking a lot for granted. More stunning still...she wasn't sure she minded.

"I just hadn't talked her into staying out here. Yet," Jackson added, his blue eyes dancing mischievously.

"Well, do so, pronto," Lilah advised as she stood on tiptoe to kiss her son's cheek. She turned to embrace Lacey, as well.

"Bye, kids." Looking every bit as pleased as his wife about the developing relationship between Jackson and Lacey, John opened the passenger door for his wife and ushered her inside. "We've got to run."

Lacey and Jackson waved as they drove off, then turned to face each other. Jackson drew in a deep breath, let it out. "You ready to crash yet?"

Lacey shook her head. She ran a fingertip down his chest experimentally and felt his muscles jump. "Experience tells me I've got several hours of adrenaline to get rid of. I am hungry, however."

"Me, too." He wrapped an arm around her waist and tucked her in close to his side. "Let's go find out what's in the kitchen." He leaned down to kiss her brow. "And then see what we can do about combining the best of both worlds."

Like everything else she owned, Jackson noted short minutes later, Lacey's jeans, boots, hat and long-sleeved denim shirt were well worn. But in this case he wouldn't change a thing. The jeans cupped her hips, and the shirt molded to her breasts. The bright blue boots added a uniquely Lacey touch. The flat-brimmed brown hat shaded her face from the morning sun. She looked sexy and at ease, and every bit as pretty as she had that morning in the operating room, when she'd pitched in and assisted him in Molly Weatherby's surgery.

They were a good team in so many ways. So good, Jackson realized as their horses topped the rise, that the thought of going on without her in his life was a daunting one. He looked over at Lacey, appreciating the play of golden sunlight on her face and hair. "I didn't expect you to know how to ride so well." But she'd turned out to be as natural in the saddle as she had been in bed.

Lacey looked out at the rolling green pastures of the McCabe ranch that were spread beneath them. For a moment she was silent, then the corners of her lips tilted up. "A year ago I didn't. Then I started taking care of Pete Hanson's eight kids. He couldn't pay me in cash, so he offered to pay me in riding lessons on his ranch. I'd always wanted to learn to ride, so every afternoon I had off, I went out to get a lesson. By the time all his kids were caught up on their shots and physical exams, I'd learned all I needed to know to get around by myself, so these days I just go whenever I can and ride."

Having found what they felt was the perfect picnic site on a shady bluff overlooking the rest of the ranch, they tethered their horses to a tree. "I've got to admit it's the one thing I miss living in the city," Jackson said, as they spread out a picnic blanket a short distance away. Lacey spread out the breakfast they'd packed. Lilah's flaky buttermilk biscuits, split and filled with thick slices of sugar-cured ham, fresh peaches, a thermos of strong hot coffee and another of icy cold milk. She bit into a peach, then licked the juice from her thumb. "Did you ride a lot as a kid?"

Reveling in the peace he felt, being here with Lacey like this, Jackson nodded. "All the time. My brothers and I were constantly trying to outdo each other, so we're all expert horsemen."

"Mmm." Lacey shot him a teasing glance. "I don't think I've ever dated a cowboy-doctor before."

Jackson winked as he unwrapped a biscuit for himself. "That makes us even, because I've never dated a city girl turned cowgirl doc, either."

They ate in silence, enjoying each other's company and the beauty of the Texas morning. "You could still have all this, you know, if you stayed here instead of Fort Worth," Lacey remarked quietly, looking like she didn't understand why he'd ever want to leave.

Jackson shrugged, as aware as Lacey was that one of them needed to change their plans for the future, if they were ever going to be together long-term, and he was beginning to want that very much. "I could buy my own ranch just outside the city, too," he said, letting her know that other options did exist.

Lacey regarded Jackson wisfully as she speared a peach slice, dripping with juice. "True."

Jackson ran the pad of his thumb across her cheek. As their eyes met, a tenderness unlike any he'd ever felt filled his heart. "I'll always be able to come back to Laramie for visits, Lacey, no matter where I live or practice medicine," he said softly, as he pressed a kiss to her hair. "And should you one day change your mind about living here—" as he hoped she would "—the same is true for you, too."

"This is the guest room." Jackson led the way into the spacious room overlooking the swimming pool. He strode past the bed and bureau and ducked his head into the adjacent bath. "There are plenty of towels, shampoo, soap." He popped back out, small rectangular shrink-wrapped package in hand. "Even a toothbrush for you to use."

Lacey accepted it gratefully. "Thanks."

"The only thing you don't have is pajamas," Jackson winked. "But don't worry. We can remedy that, too." He dashed out, returned seconds later with a man's cotton shirt in hand. As he moved lazily toward her, Lacey found she couldn't take her eyes off him. The khaki twill shirt he had on molded softly to the muscled contours of his chest and shoulders. His faded jeans clung to his legs and lower torso like a lover's caress. His handsome face bore the golden glow of the morning sun and a hint of sun burned pink across his cheeks and nose. Just looking at him, Lacey felt her heartbeat speed up.

"Yours?" Lacey asked as he dropped it on the bureau.

Jackson's eyes held hers as he swiftly closed the distance between them and wrapped his arms around her waist. "You're not sleeping in any man's shirt but mine."

Lacey grinned. It was so intimate, standing here,

talking with him. Just as the morning had been. "Getting a tad possessive, aren't we?" she quipped.

"You bet!"

There was no doubt from the way he'd been talking that he was beginning to make long-range plans for them. And while there was nothing she'd like better than to spend her future loving Jackson, Lacey couldn't help but be a little concerned about the one-sidedness of Jackson's plans. She'd known from the beginning that he was very intent on protecting his own interests. She just didn't want it to be at her expense.

He drew her into his arms, felt her sudden stiffness. "What's wrong?"

Leery of falling in love again with a man who was only going to leave her in the end, Lacey said nothing. Jackson slid a hand beneath her chin and guided her face up to his. "You've been quiet as a mouse all morning, and it's not just fatigue, so don't even try running that one by me."

Hand to his chest, Lacey stepped away from him and stood looking out the window at the flowers edging the backyard. "Last night it seemed like the most natural thing in the world for us to be together and make love."

Wordlessly, Jackson gathered her in his arms, intuitively giving her the comfort she needed. "It was right and natural and beautiful."

Lacey laid her head against his shoulder and leaned against him, loving his warmth and his strength. She released a ragged breath and, knowing she owed it to him to be honest with him, forced herself to continue. "I just can't help but wonder if we aren't fooling ourselves." Drawing another deep breath, she forced herself to meet his eyes. "This week has been so intense, from the moment I jumped out of that cake and you laid eyes on me."

Hooking his thumbs beneath her chin, he tilted her face up to his. "You can say that again."

"But it's not the way our real lives are, either."

"I don't know about that." He kissed her gently, his tongue mating with hers. "I can easily imagine you jumping out of another cake and having just as good a time as you had the first time."

Realizing they had to get this potential problem out in the open where they could deal with it, Lacey continued, "We have to be realistic here. The fact of the matter is my life is here, and once you go on to Fort Worth, you may very well meet someone else and decide you'd rather be with them than me."

"First of all, no one is going to replace you in my affections, Lacey," Jackson told her gruffly as his fingertips flattened on her spine, bringing her as close as their clothes would allow. "Second, there's no reason for us to go borrowing trouble, worrying about the future now." His lips traced the shell of her ear, the soft slope of her neck, leaving her feeling deliciously distraught. His blue eyes dark with passion, he brought her back to him and kissed her with tantalizing slowness. Lacey would've liked nothing better than to spend the entire afternoon and evening in bed with Jackson, but she knew from experience once she got into bed with him, she would not want to get out.

She sighed, the mixture of overwhelming emotion and confusion she was feeling making her feel like she had the weight of the world on her shoulders. She traced her fingers across the width of his shoulders. "I might agree with you if I hadn't been this route before."

Jackson tensed, as he always did when he didn't understand her. Hands cupping her shoulders, he drew back so he could see her face. "What are you talking about?" he asked softly.

Lacey knew she had to tell him, no matter how humiliated she felt recounting the details of her failed romance. Otherwise he would never understand. "When I was a first-year resident, I met and became involved with this star athlete at the medical center, Bart Dobson."

"The pro football player?"

Lacey nodded. "He was recovering from a career-threatening shoulder injury, and I'd heard he was really discouraged. I was on a surgical rotation so I stopped in to see him and gave him some encouragement, and it helped him. He asked me to come by again and see him. So I did. And one thing led to another and we started dating." Lacey paused and shook her head, remembering the hours she had spent with him, encouraging him in his physical therapy. "I thought I was in love with him. I thought he loved me and was going to ask me to marry him. But when he made a better-than-expected recovery and got the word he could go back to playing pro ball, well, it became apparent that I didn't fit in his life any more than he fit in mine, and we broke up." *Just like you might decide I no longer fit in your life.*

Jackson studied her for a long moment, then asked flatly, "You broke up or he dumped you?"

Lacey flushed. Leave it to Jackson not to sugarcoat anything even for the sake of her pride, she thought wryly. "He dumped me."

Jackson continued to regard her laconically. "That's when you bought all the new clothes for yourself— when you were dating him?"

Aware he was still cataloging her every emotion, Lacey nodded and stepped away from him once again. "I tried to be something I wasn't. I wanted to fit in his life. I wanted to be what he wanted me to be, and in the process I lost sight of the real me." Shoving her hands in the pockets of her jeans, she paced the length of the bedroom and back. "I don't want to do that again. I don't want to fool myself into believing that there is any way on earth that you and I are actually going to end up together after this month-long vacation of yours ends. 'Cause it just isn't going to happen, and I know that, even if you won't let yourself admit it just yet."

"I won't admit it," Jackson pointed out, his sensual mouth thinning once again, "because it isn't true."

Lacey released a long, exasperated breath and propped both her hands on her hips. "Jackson, what we've had—what we're having—is a fling," she explained, unable for one second longer to contain her impatience with his single-minded attitude. "Granted," Lacey continued sarcastically, striding nearer, "it's a wonderful fling. But it's still nothing more than a fling, and we need to keep that in mind." They needed to protect their hearts here as best they could! "So no more talk about the future or me someday moving to the city, too!"

Jackson hauled her into his arms and held her

against the length of him. "Listen to me, Lacey," he said gruffly, running his hands through the tousled layers of her hair, smoothing it away from her face. "You are more than a fling to me."

Hearing the hurt in his voice gave Lacey pause. "You say that now," she protested huskily.

"And I'll say it tomorrow, too," Jackson said as he bent his head to hers. Studying her all the while, he lowered his lips slowly, inevitably, to hers and continued huskily, "I want you to be my woman, Lacey. And mine alone."

His woman. Lacey wanted to be that and so much more. But she was afraid that by demanding so little of themselves they were setting themselves up for hurt. Heart pounding, she splayed her hands across his chest, and focused her eyes on the beautiful blue of his. "Jackson, I—"

He cut her off with a deliberate shake of his head. "Stop talking, Lacey." Before she could do so much as take a breath, his lips found the soft, sensitive spot behind her ear and trailed down her neck. His hands shifted down her spine, fitting her against him until she no longer knew where his body ended and hers began.

She told herself to fight him—fight this—but with shimmers of almost unbearable sensation sweeping through her—and his hands urging her closer still, it was an impossible task.

"I want you, Lacey. You want me," Jackson whispered against her hair. With his thumb he traced the delicate shape of her lips. "For now, that's all we need to know. All we need to worry about."

One hand still held her close; the other moved to cup

her chin. Tilting her face up to his, he captured her lips with his in a kiss that was hot and wet and so unbearably sweet and tender it had her shuddering even as she swept her tongue into his mouth and demanded more.

Maybe he was right, she thought, as he merged their lips in one long steamy kiss. Maybe this was all they needed to think about today. Heaven knew she'd had very little time to play, growing up, she thought as she arched against him, her breasts pressing against the solid warmth of his chest, her tummy cradling the hardness of his sex. Her adulthood thus far had been the same way—all duty and responsibility and so little fun. Maybe Jackson was right, she thought as his own control slipped a bit. Maybe it was time she found— and took—the pleasure where she could. Heaven knew, a love affair this passionate was not likely to happen again. Not in her lifetime.

His heart thudding as heavily as hers, Jackson danced her backward to the bed and, hands shifting to her waist, set her down to sit on the edge. He paused to kiss her again, arousing her with slow, certain strokes. When she had melted against him in abject surrender, he knelt at her feet. "What are you doing?" Lacey asked breathlessly.

Jackson grinned up at her and paused to kiss her chastely. "Got to get these off." He slid one hand beneath the heel of the vibrant blue cowboy boot—the other possessively cupped the back of her blue-jeaned knee. He tugged once and then again, to no avail. The tight-fitting leather didn't budge.

Laughing softly, for she often had trouble getting her boots off, too, Lacey leaned forward, curving both hands over his shoulders to steady herself and provide some resistance. "Okay, cowboy, one more time."

Jackson's lips—still wet from her kisses—curved upward. His eyes danced with a mischievous light. "I like the sound of that," he murmured sexily as he tried again, giving the boot a harder tug. This time it came off. Grinning, he tossed it aside and shifted positions slightly to remove the other. When he'd tugged it off it lay with the other.

"Okay, now yours," Lacey said, determined that this time they'd maintain the same pace.

"Not so fast." Hands on her thighs, Jackson kept her from getting up. He moved into the apex of her thighs, and Lacey's breath did a little jig in her chest.

"I want you naked first." Jackson's hands went to the button fly on her jeans. Deftly he worked the buttons free, then parted the worn edges of her fly. "I knew I'd get to see these eventually," he teased, smoothing his hands across her white cotton panties again and again.

The next thing Lacey knew, her jeans were coming off. To her increasing frustration the panties were staying on. "Now what do you have in mind?" Lacey asked breathlessly as he peeled her jeans past her ankles and dropped them on the floor beside the bed.

"Just this." Jackson unbuttoned his way up her denim shirt, not stopping until he had undone all those, too. Again he parted the edges of the cloth and stripped the shirt past her wrists. He dropped it to the floor, to rest beside her jeans, leaving Lacey clad only in a thin white undershirt, panties and socks. Taking her wrists in hand, he held her there, sitting on the edge of the bed in the shimmering mid-morning sun.

Still sitting on the floor in front of her, he leaned back on his haunches to look his fill. As erotic moments passed, Lacey's heart pounded all the harder.

"You are so beautiful," he whispered.

And aroused, Lacey thought, aware it was all she could do to sit still. He hadn't even touched her yet, and her panties were damp with the evidence of her desire, her breasts aching, her nipples taut and straining against the cloth and yearning to be touched.

There was no reason this had to be so incredibly sexy, and yet…it was.

"So where do you want me to start?" Still holding her wrists against the mattress on either side of her, Jackson leaned forward and lightly kissed her knees.

Lacey gulped, and this time she did shift, just a little, as Jackson moved in a little closer between her spread thighs, his body hard and masculine against hers.

"What do you mean?" she asked huskily, afraid she knew.

"Do you want me to start here?" Jackson stroked his way up her thigh with his tongue, stopping just short of the feminine heart of her. "Or here?" He went to her other thigh and stroked his way back down to her knee.

At the light, butterfly touch of his tongue on her skin, it was all Lacey could do not to groan.

"Tell me, Lacey," he prodded softly. "Tell me what you want."

Knowing she was caught up in something too powerful and wonderful to fight, Lacey arched toward him wantonly and released a shuddering breath. She had never imagined she could surrender to any man this way, never imagined she could need this way. What the heck, she thought, she might as well tell him. Because today was for loving him. And allowing him to love her back. Knowing there was no need to rush, no need to deny the feelings swirling around in her heart, no need to worry about tomorrow today, she looked into his eyes and said, "I want...everything."

His eyes lit up, the rigidness of his arousal pressing against the front of his jeans. "Everything?" he asked hoarsely.

"You can think of, and them some," she added helpfully.

"All right," he whispered playfully, pleased. "A woman after my own heart." He kissed the top of her knee. And the other.

The last of her inhibitions melting away with astonishing speed, Lacey closed her eyes as the telltale moisture gathered between her thighs and her muscles trembled and tensed. She was in over her head and sinking fast. "Jackson?"

"Hmm?" He was working his way up the inside of her thigh again, loving and discovering every sweet, fragrant inch of her.

"Do you think—" Lacey gasped as he did a sexy but frustrating detour and went back to the inside of the other thigh again. She hitched in a breath as he showed her just how good their loving could be. "Do you think we could go a little faster?"

"I see what you mean." Jackson shifted her wrists behind her and shackled them there with one hand. Using his free hand, he moved the elastic waistband of her panties down, just far enough to reveal her navel.

He dipped his tongue inside, circling the indentation. Again and again and again, he kissed her like he meant to have her, and this time Lacey did groan. "Want something?" he teased.

Lacey shut her eyes. Oh heavens, yes. "Higher," she directed hoarsely. Moving her tank-style undershirt aside, he found her breasts, first with his lips, then his hands, then both, keeping it up until she moaned.

"Lower," she whispered, trembling from head to toe. And he obliged, sliding down once again to kneel between her thighs. She cupped his head in her hands as he kissed her through the soft cotton cloth, teasing and caressing until her entire body was melting against him in boneless pleasure.

The next thing she knew, he had pushed her back to the center of the bed and lowered her so she was lying on her side. As he stretched out next to her, an expression of almost primal possessiveness on his face, his tall hard body facing hers, she shifted closer, welcoming his warmth and his strength. "Am I still calling the shots?" she murmured sexily, divesting herself of her clothes. His eyes on hers, Jackson made a low, affirmative sound in the back of his throat, letting her know this was indeed so.

"Then these," Lacey directed, unbuttoning his shirt, then his jeans, "have both definitely got to come off."

"Bossy, aren't you?" Jackson teased as he let her have her way.

Lacey swiftly divested him of his shirt, boots and jeans. "When it comes to getting what I want, you bet," Lacey sighed as she ran her hands through the thick mat of hair on his chest. She loved the way the crisp curling hairs and warm smooth skin felt beneath her fingers.

Hooking her fingers beneath the elastic, she eased off his black bikini briefs and watched his considerable erection spring free. Just that suddenly, he situated himself between her thighs. "I think we're ready now," he said.

Aware she hadn't begun to get started making love to him the way she wanted to make love to him, Lacey protested, "But I haven't yet—"

"You will," he murmured against her mouth, kissing her again and again as his hands palmed her breasts and he brought his whole body into contact with hers. "We both will. When the time is right. For now, this is what I want." Rolling onto his back, he shifted her over top of him, so her knees were straddling his waist, her hands braced on his shoulders. "This," he said, his eyes full of love, as he ever so slowly and sensually pushed all the way inside her, "is what I need."

Her heart filling with all the sweetness of the moment and the love she felt in her heart, Lacey took all of his hot, hard length inside her and held him there—then drew herself up so she was once again on her knees. As she added a soul-searching kiss and the caressing pressure of her hands, the effect on Jackson was all she could have hoped for and more.

Jackson moaned and surged against her, their ragged breaths meshing as one. "Lacey...sweetheart..."

Shaking with her need for him, Lacey kissed him passionately and repeated the motion all over again.

The gliding sensation of hot wet silk almost more than he could bear, Jackson caught Lacey's hips and forced her down, letting her do for him, with the most feminine part of her, what he had already done for her. Hands on her waist, he urged her up, then guided her down with rapidly escalating pleasure. Over and over again until he too lost the control he had imposed upon himself and reached the pinnacle of release. And suddenly she was there, too, kissing him deeply, shuddering, her euphoric cries mingling with his.

Afterward, Jackson held Lacey close. As she rested her head on his chest and cuddled against him, he wrapped his arms around her and held her tight. Aware he'd never wanted a woman this completely, he thought about how wonderful it felt to have her in his arms. He wished they had more time. A month wasn't long to work everything out, he thought, as he skimmed her body with his fingers, filling his hands with her soft, hot flesh. He also wished Lacey wasn't so skittish when it came to commitment or expressing her feelings for him.

But given a little time…the love he was feeling… and the way she had surrendered herself to him— They could do it. He was sure of it. Meantime, they had their passion, their sizzling-hot kisses and tender caresses filled with longing, to bind them together. At least for now, she was his. Was it enough? Jackson wondered, as he rolled so that she was beneath him and he began to make love to her all over again.

Given the circumstances, it had to be.

Chapter 10

"Good news for you, Molly, my darling," Lacey said as she entered the little girl's hospital room the following day.

Five-year-old Molly—who was cuddled in her mother's arms, her Teddy Beddy tucked beneath her chin—grinned from ear to ear. Her lively eyes danced. "I get to go home today!" she announced happily.

Lacey put her chart on the table and perched on the edge of Molly's hospital bed. "How did you know that?" Lacey lifted Molly's gown and checked the incision site. To her satisfaction, all looked to be healing nicely.

Molly peered down at her tummy, too, then looked back at Lacey. "My fever is all gone and I'm not sick to my tummy anymore—it just hurts when I move around." Molly handed Teddy Beddy to her mother and demonstrated.

"That's from the surgery," Lacey said, pleased to see Molly sitting up so well already. "And that'll be gone before you know it," she reassured. "In fact, the more you move around, the sooner the soreness will go away. So anytime you feel like getting up and walking around a bit, you let your mommy know, and she can help you. Okay, pumpkin?" Lacey playfully tweaked the end of Molly's nose.

"Okay." Molly beamed.

"Meantime I'll get the paperwork started and get a wheelchair up here, and you can get out of here today, how about that?"

"Yeah!" Molly cheered, looking happy about that.

"We were hoping that would be the case," Patricia Weatherby said.

"Well, it is." Lacey smiled, noting without surprise that Patricia looked as relieved as Lacey that Molly's post-op had gone as smoothly as her surgery and she was finally en route to a complete recovery.

Jackson had done a wonderful job with the surgery, Lacey thought. And the Weatherbys weren't the only ones around who were pleased with his skill as a physician and a surgeon. Rafe Marshall—the principal of the elementary school—was also recovering nicely, as were the rest of the patients Jackson had operated on that week. She'd been hoping, as word got out and patients started lining up to see him, that Jackson would realize how immensely satisfying it could be to practice medicine here, too, and change his mind about staying. But so far—to her disappointment—that did not seem to be happening.

"And we have even more good news for you," Margaret added, coming in to join the group. She was dressed in her pink volunteer smock, a starched white blouse and white shoes. Acting both as the mayor's wife and the first lady of Laramie and the president of the Pink Ladies, Margaret continued kindly, "I know you two are going to need a place to stay until you get back on your feet, so I've put in a word here and there and came up with this." Margaret reached into the pocket of her volunteer smock and withdrew a small notepad, covered with neat handwriting. "One of our city councilmen is looking to rent a house he owns on Elm Street. It's small—two bedrooms, a bath, eat-in kitchen and living room—but convenient, and close to the elementary school, should you and Molly decide to stay here next fall. And here's a list of businesses currently needing help. The one I'd recommend you check out first is the position with the Laramie Chamber of Commerce. The pay isn't all that great, but the hours are flexible, the office relaxed enough that you can take Molly to work with you if you want. And if not, I have a list of excellent sitters there, too."

Patricia—who'd already had a discussion with the hospital business office and worked out a payment plan for Molly's hospital bill—teared up. "I don't know what to say. I can't believe y'all are being so good to us— virtual strangers."

"That's the kind of place Laramie is," Margaret said gently.

"And why my mom and I moved here," Lacey agreed as she and Margaret exchanged smiles. "When it comes to downright friendliness and caring about your fellow human being there's nothing like a small town in Texas. It beats the big city every time."

"I'll say." Patricia wiped a tear from her eye while Molly cuddled contentedly in her arms.

"In the meantime you can count on my mom and me and Margaret and everyone else here for continued help," Laccy said gently.

"I don't know how to thank y'all," Patricia said in a choked voice.

"You don't have to thank us," Lacey said, meaning it. It had been enough to be able to help.

Margaret nodded, adding, as she clamped a comforting arm around Patricia Weatherby's shoulder, "Just do a good turn for someone else when you have a chance, and we'll be all square."

Lacey was on the phone with Seth Schofield when Jackson emerged from surgery a few hours later and knocked on her office door. Still cradling the receiver to her ear, she waved him in and wrapped up her conversation warmly. "That's great, Seth. I am so pleased. And everyone else on the search committee will be, too. Right. I'll have the relocation Realtor get in touch with you immediately. Right. Look forward to seeing you then."

"He accepted the job?" Jackson asked, as soon as Lacey had hung up the phone.

Lacey nodded, noting that Jackson did not look any happier than she felt about Seth taking the spot that had once been earmarked for Jackson. She'd been hoping Jackson would be the one permanently joining the hospital staff, not Seth. But it hadn't worked out that way and she had to get over it. It didn't mean Jackson couldn't eventually come to Laramie, too, and practice medicine. With the amount of elective surgeries currently being shipped off to other hospitals, the surrounding community could easily provide plenty of work for two or three surgeons. And Jackson had to know that, too.

Thinking how good Jackson looked in scrubs, his dark hair damp and touchably mussed, Lacey sat back in her chair. Glancing over at him affectionately, she continued filling him in on the latest developments. "Seth won't officially start holding office hours for two more weeks, but he'll be in the area and has agreed to cover with emergency services in the interim. So," Lacey continued lightly, "as of tomorrow evening you're off the hook. Our agreement is null and void. You won't have to be on call here anymore."

"Good." Jackson flexed his broad shoulders restlessly. 'Cause there's something I have to tell you, too." Jackson shut the door behind him then. He closed the distance between them with long, lazy strides, then sat on the edge of her desk, looking like he was savoring their nearness as much as she was. "I just had a call from the group practice I'm joining in Fort Worth." He continued to regard her with an intensity that was both casual and unnerving. "They need me right away."

"How right away?" Lacey asked in the same easy tone, as she tried to ignore the sudden rapid beating of her heart.

"Monday." Jackson picked up a paperweight from her desk and turned it end over end. "That gives us the weekend." He put the paperweight down and rested his hand on his thigh, next to his knee. "I don't have to leave till Sunday night."

The knowledge that Jackson was leaving Laramie so much sooner than expected hit Lacey like a blow to the heart and left her feeling that she couldn't breathe, that life would never be the same again. But he was taking this all in stride, behaving as if he had expected their love affair to come to a much-sooner-than-expected end all along, Lacey noted with despair as a disturbing sense of déjà vu swept through her. Hadn't she been this route before, with Bart? Once he'd gotten word that the team wanted him back, and the medical green light to play, he'd been out of her life like a bat out of hell. And now, years later, Jackson was doing the very same thing. And she—fool that she was—had chosen to ignore the inevitable. Once they'd made love, she'd thought—she'd hoped—everything would change. Obviously, Lacey thought bitterly, that was not the case.

Trying hard to mask her hurt, she moved lithely to her feet. Turning deliberately away from him, she quipped, "Why put off till tomorrow what you can do today?"

Jackson manacled a hand around her wrist and tugged her back to stand between his spread legs before she could move away. "Because I don't want to leave you."

Lacey didn't want that, either. But it didn't make any difference. "But you're going to leave me, anyway," Lacey reminded, as she smiled tightly and continued to try to take his news in stride.

"Not necessarily," Jackson replied quietly. He

stroked the length of her arms with his palms and pinned her in place with his sexy gaze. He was close enough she could smell the aftershave clinging to his jaw and the minty freshness of his breath. Her senses swam at his nearness even as she lamented Jackson's stubbornness and the no-win situation they found themselves in.

"We make a good team," Jackson continued, looking for a moment as if he were savoring her nearness as much as she was his. "You know it and I know it."

Lacey swallowed hard and tried not to let her heart—or her patently unrealistic hopes for the future—get ahead of her this time. "Medically, we did what was right for Molly Weatherby—"

"I agree, but I'm not talking about just that." Jackson twined his fingers with hers and rested them on his thighs. "I'm talking about us, too."

Lacey looked down at their clasped hands. She could feel the heat and strength of his legs emanating through the soft cotton scrubs.

Her heart quaked as she thought about all that was at stake here, and she turned her glance up to his. "Then stay," she implored him softly. "We could always use two surgeons here. There'd be plenty of work for you both."

Jackson's lips compressed. The light went out of his eyes as swiftly as it had appeared. "I've already told you why I can't do that," he reminded her stonily.

"Right," Lacey said sarcastically. She pushed away from him in frustration and began to pace her office. "You want to be the best and live the good life you've earned, to the hilt. And the only way you can do both those things—the only way you'll know you are the best surgeon around—is if you practice in a highly competitive, very lucrative big-city practice."

Jackson remained where he was, ignoring the slight tinge of derision underlying her words. "The professional opportunities and challenges in Fort Worth are unlimited for us both, Lacey."

Lacey shook her head, deciding to deal with their situation realistically, even if he wouldn't. "I'm not interested in joining a high profile medical practice." The truth was they didn't want the same things in life. Never had. Never would.

Jackson caught her arm when she would have stalked past him, and swung her around to face him, so swiftly she collided with his chest. "It doesn't matter to me whether you work in a private practice or a free clinic," he said, pulling her into the warm, hard cradle of his legs once again. "All I care about is us being close enough—geographically—to see each other on a regular basis."

Lacey raised her chin. "You've thought it all out."

Jackson sighed. "There hasn't been much time but I've tried."

And yet, Lacey thought, even more upset that he hadn't mentioned marriage or even the hint of it. He hadn't even told her he loved her. He had said he enjoyed sleeping with her and wanted to continue to do so without being under the watchful—and she admitted to herself reluctantly, inevitably disapproving—eyes of their families. Not to mention the entire town where he'd grown up!

Jackson didn't know it, but his let's-continue-seeing-each-other-but-only-on-my-terms edict was eerily similar to the one Bart gave her when he wanted to go back to the pro football, womanizing life-style he'd had before his injury and subsequent meeting of and involvement with her. It had been Bart's way of not dealing with the fact he'd unconsciously used her to liven up what had otherwise been an insufferably dull and lonely and confusing time for him. It had been Bart's way of easing out of a relationship that never should have started, in the most-painless-for-him way possible. Unfortunately, doing it that way had multiplied her own pain and humiliation tenfold, Lacey recalled. She didn't want to go through that agony of seeing Jackson's interest in her fade an inch at a time. She didn't want him making love to her if his heart and soul weren't in it. She didn't want him hanging around guiltily while he tried to figure out how and when to actually end things between them.

No, the simple fact of the matter was she had been dumped once, by a man who'd turned her whole life upside-down and persuaded her to give herself heart and soul to him. So what, if what she felt for Jackson was a thousand times stronger than the attraction she'd felt for Bart? The bottom line was she didn't want to be dumped again. Not now. Not later. But if the worst happened and she was going to be dumped, for whatever reasons, Lacey thought determinedly, then by golly, it was going to be on her terms.

"I have a better idea," Lacey said sweetly. Her temper flared and combined with her hurt pride as she stepped aside. "Let's call the physical side of our relationship quits now and just be friends."

* * *

Jackson had sworn he would never again stand there with a ring burning a hole in his pocket, getting ready to ask a woman to marry him who ultimately had no interest in marrying him. But here he was. A diamond engagement ring pinned to the hem of his shirt awaiting a most memorable delivery, getting ready for what was likely to be one of the defining moments in his life. Only to find that fate had thrown a monkey wrench into all his plans.

The last time he had just backed off and said to hell with it, and for good reason—the woman he'd thought he loved, and later discovered he had really only lusted after—had betrayed him. This time the situation was different. But he still had time to make her understand they couldn't just throw everything away. Not after all they had shared.

"Lacey, I love you."

She tensed all the more and looked at him as if it were too little too late. Gone was the contented woman who had left his bed that morning. Her face wore a grim look that not even their night of incredible love-making could erase. "I know you think you do," Lacey said stiffly. There was no missing the boiling fury and resentment in her green eyes. "At least for now…"

"For forever," Jackson corrected as she pushed away from him once again. He just wished he'd said it sooner, before he'd found out he had to leave.

"Bart said that, too," Lacey shot back bitterly. She shrugged her shoulders negligently, clearly not believing a word he had just said. "I know he even meant it at the time, too."

Jackson shot to his feet. "What does that have to do with us?" he demanded gruffly.

Lacey planted her hands on her hips. She regarded him with mounting exasperation, spelling it out for him bluntly, "It means, our current feelings for each other aside, there is no guarantee that things would work out in the long run, or that you'll always feel that way about me, or me about you, or that circumstances and life won't get in the way of what we've had."

Jackson released a long, frustrated breath. He wasn't used to having his emotions thrown in his face! He didn't like being backed into a corner, either, with her demands, her insistence that he do everything her way—stay and practice medicine in Laramie right alongside her—or hit the highway. "The realities of life have already gotten in the way." Jackson advanced on her slowly, deliberately. Telling himself the situation was bad—but not unsalvageable and wouldn't be unless he lost his head—he took her rigid body in his arms.

Her slender shoulders stiffened beneath his staying grip. "Exactly my point," Lacey volleyed back dryly, looking as if she felt even more betrayed.

"It doesn't mean we can't deal with it," Jackson said, aware that the thought of a life without her was more than he could bear.

Cupping a hand on the nape of her neck, Jackson tried to make her look at him, but she wouldn't and she wasn't listening, either.

"That's what I'm trying to do here—be honest with you and with me!" Lacey shoved away from him and went on lecturing him as if he hadn't spoken at all.

She sighed and ran her hands through her mane of silky, honey-blond hair before she continued in a low voice that was bleak and utterly defeated. "It was fun while it lasted, Jackson. And I'll never forget it, and I'll never regret being with you the way I have been this week, but we have to be honest with each other," she continued in a low, tortured voice that made him feel all the guiltier. "A fling is all this was ever going to be or ever will be," she said flatly, looking as if she was struggling not to cry. Her hands were balled into fists at her sides, and after a moment she regarded him with a surprising lack of emotion and said, "And that being the case, I think we should just deal with it."

Aware he had never wanted to hold on to something—or someone—more in his life Jackson spoke with exaggerated civility. "I get what you're trying to tell me in your roundabout way," he said gruffly, doing his best to forget the way she had pulled out all the stops—jumping out of a cake and stripping down to a bikini to meet him. Deliberately he put aside the sweet and tender way she had given herself to him, not once but again and again. Her passionate surrender had been…and still most likely was…a means to an end for her. Only his ego—and his swiftly growing feelings for her—had gotten in the way of him seeing Lacey's actions for what they really were. Well, no more, he thought angrily.

"Good. I'm glad you get it!" Lacey retorted in a low, deadpan voice. "Now kindly explain it to me."

"It's simple." Jackson shrugged his broad shoulders uncaringly. "You used me!"

Lacey's eyes widened. Her green eyes sparkled with

angry lights. "Now, wait just a minute, cowboy," she fumed, advancing on him. "Don't you have this just a little backward?"

Jackson shook his head grimly. He didn't think so. And as much as he was loath to admit it, he figured it might do him good to acknowledge what had really happened between them, to keep it from happening again—with Lacey or any other woman. "You never would have spent so much time with me if you hadn't needed me to fill in as surgeon at the hospital," he told her flatly. Just like Amelia would never have spent so much time pursuing him if she hadn't needed to gain access to his brother Wade. The only difference was, when cornered, Amelia was a little more honest about it. Damn it all, he wondered in deepening frustration, when was he ever going to learn?

"I don't deny the hospital's need of your services was initially what brought us together," Lacey reminded him coolly.

"So I have just one question for you," Jackson said, wanting suddenly to hurt her and disappoint her the way she had hurt him. "When and if Seth Schofield finds the social scene around here slow going, will you sleep with him to help keep him happy, too?"

The second the words were out Jackson knew he had crossed the line. But the passionate slap across the face that he expected never came. Lacey made no effort to advance on him or hurl herself into his arms. She merely gave him a long look, her expression stony with resolve. "I think you'd better leave before you say or do anything else you'll regret," she told him dispassionately.

"I already have!" Jackson slammed out the door.

Unfortunately he didn't know yet if it could be undone.

"That's it," Lacey said as she carried the last suitcase of their things into their rented house on Elm Street and helped them get settled.

Patricia and Molly beamed at Lacey and her mother gratefully. "I can't thank you enough," Patricia said.

Isabel smiled and gave the other mother a hug. "We were happy to help."

Lacey and her mother walked back out to Lacey's car. They got in and drove home in silence. "Well, now all I have to do is go back to the hospital and get my stuff and move it back to the apartment and we'll be all set," Lacey said determinedly as they entered the bakery kitchen via the back door. "Life can return to normal." *And I can stop moping about one very sexy Texas surgeon.*

"Actually, honey, I've been wanting to talk to you about that." Isabel brought out milk and a plate of cookies.

"Don't tell me you decided you like living without me," Lacey joked as she curled up on a stool opposite her mother.

"Actually, I think it is time you moved on," Isabel said with a frown.

"You're kidding."

Isabel took Lacey's hands gently in hers. "Honey, you're thirty years old!"

And nowhere near married or happily settled down, Lacey thought unhappily, the way she'd wanted to be by this point in her life. "You don't have to remind me of that, Mom," Lacey retorted crisply, taking a big gulp of icy cold milk. "I know how old I am."

Isabel looked at her compassionately. "But do you know how the postbankruptcy years have affected you?" she queried gently, looking as distressed as Lacey felt.

Lacey sat back, waited.

Isabel continued to study her. Her expression gentled even more, then turned to one of understanding mixed with pity. "I think you've become afraid. You still feel that at any moment the floor might give way beneath you the way it did when your father died and left us with that massive debt and we lost everything and found ourselves on the street."

Lacey was silent for moments, as was her mother. "I admit it was a rough time," Lacey said finally.

Isabel lifted a hand. "Let's be honest. Our world was turned upside down. And we survived by holding on to each other as tightly as we could."

Lacey swallowed around the growing lump of emotion in her throat. "I'm not going to stop loving you, Mom."

"Oh, honey, I'm not asking you to stop loving me!" Isabel replied urgently. "I'm asking you to think about your future—about how you're going to go on without me, as one day you'll have to. And the only way you're going to be able to do that is if you have other people in your life to love."

Lacey ignored the fact her mother had struck a chord, and she put on her bravest face. "I have lots of friends," she countered quietly.

Isabel leaned forward urgently. "I'm talking family here, Lacey. A husband. Kids."

Lacey's eyes misted over with tears. "Don't you think I want that?" she demanded miserably. "Don't you think I want Jackson?"

Isabel sighed. "I think you're afraid to even wish for that, much less enact a plan that will make it a reality instead of some far-off dream. And I think that, more than anything else, is what is keeping you here while Jackson goes off to practice medicine in Fort Worth."

Finding herself unable to eat a bite, Lacey hopped off her stool and paced the room badtemperedly. "Mom, I love you, but you are really out of line here."

Unfortunately, Isabel didn't think so. "I know you've only known him for a week or so, Lacey."

Lacey stopped pacing and spun around to face her. "Now you're on to something!"

"But I've seen the way you look at Jackson McCabe, Lacey," Isabel continued unperturbed. "And I've seen the way he looks at you. And that's why, honey, I'm asking you to move out and find your own place!"

"Dr. McCabe, I really need your full attention here if we're going to get finished today."

Jackson looked up from the carpet samples spread in front of him. He realized he had been staring at them nonstop for fifteen minutes, and he hadn't heard a word the young and gorgeous interior decorator had said. In fact, if she hadn't just tapped him on the shoulder, he wouldn't even have remembered she was in the room. "Look, uh, Miss—"

"Smith…Sally," the decorator said unhappily.

Jackson frowned. "Miss Smith. For the hundredth time, I really don't care what style desk I have, never mind what color the carpet or wall coverings are in this office. So just—I don't know—pick out whatever you think'll do and go with it," Jackson finished curtly.

"I'm confused. I was told you were—are—a man with very definite, discriminating taste."

Only when it comes to potential wives. In that category there was only one woman who would do, and that woman didn't want him. "Well, I'm not now," Jackson said gruffly, turning away. Was it him, or was it suffocating in here? "So just do what you have to do to satisfy the partners, and don't worry about me."

"But I do worry," Sally Smith said softly, edging all the closer. "I want you to be happy here. Everyone who's in any way associated with the group practice does."

It was a come-on, and a rather blatant one at that. In the old days, the preLacey days, Jackson probably would have taken her up on the come-hither look in her eyes and gone out to dinner or a movie with her and had a few laughs. It probably wouldn't have led to much of anything, but they would have enjoyed each other's company and said adieu, no big deal. But these days, since Lacey, he couldn't even consider it. Damn it all, anyway. The woman hadn't just ruined his life, she'd ruined his ability to enjoy women casually, too.

"Just figure out something that goes with what everyone else already has and do it. I'll be happy with the results. I promise." Jackson gently guided her out the door, just as Margaret Ferguson-Moore was headed in.

Jackson narrowed his eyes at his former classmate

and Laramie's resident busybody and mayor's wife. "I thought I left you behind in Laramie."

"I'm like a piece of chewing gun on your shoe. You'll never get rid of me."

Margaret shut the door behind them.

"Is this going to take long?" Jackson continued cantankerously.

"Heavens!" Margaret rolled her eyes and dropped into a chair. She leaned forward in a confiding manner. "I hope not. I have a whole town of people back there to oversee, you know."

It was Jackson's turn to roll his eyes. "So what's this about?" he demanded gruffly. "Did Seth Schofield not work out?" And why was he hoping this was the case? Jackson wondered fervently, surprised at his sudden lack of charity.

"Actually—" Margaret smiled as she touched a hand to her bouffant red hair "—he's working out beautifully. Lacey said the patients who'd been putting off procedures are already signing up right and left to see him."

They'd been doing that for him, too, Jackson thought, at least until he up and left. He nodded with a great deal more politeness than he felt. "Glad to hear it," he drawled.

Margaret sent him a sly look. "I imagine you want to hear about Lacey, too."

Jackson's bad mood took a thunderous turn for the worst. "Actually, Margaret," he said grimly, "I do not want to hear about Lacey at all."

Margaret smiled. "Too bad," she chirped right back, "because I'm going to tell you. She's miserable, too."

Good, he thought with an even more surprising lack of charity, then that makes us even. Jackson slid his hands in his pockets and fingered the velvet ring box he was still carrying around with him constantly. Why? He didn't know. He should have taken the ring back to the jeweler's days ago.

"What—no comment?" Margaret prodded.

Jackson shrugged. "There's nothing to say."

Margaret shook her head in a disparaging manner. "You and Lacey really are two of a kind. She won't talk, either."

Jackson felt the first ray of hope. But not about to get persuaded into making a fool of himself all over again, he said with as much indifference as he could muster, "Doesn't surprise me."

Margaret continued to study Jackson with a critical gaze. "You know, of course, Lacey's mother kicked her out of the apartment?"

Jackson did a double take. "Isabel?" Surely there was some mistake! Isabel loved Lacey more than life! Jackson would stake his own life on that!

"Yep." Margaret lifted both hands, palms up, on either side of her. "I was stunned, too." Margaret continued in a stage whisper, "Lacey suspects there's a man involved—that her mother's finally ready for a romance of her own—but right now she has no idea who it might be."

Isabel in a romance? Jackson liked the sound of that. "Good for her," Jackson said.

"Of course, that leaves Lacey more alone than ever," Margaret continued.

That, Jackson didn't like. But not about to let Margaret the town crier know how he felt, he merely shrugged his broad shoulders listlessly. "That's her choice to make."

"The thing is—" Margaret stood, her manner suddenly becoming much more combative "—I don't think that's the choice Lacey would have made if you hadn't blown it with her, Jackson McCabe!"

"Me!" Jackson echoed, guilt assailing him anew. He clamped two hands across his chest. "What did I do?"

"I think the question is—" Margaret replied just as deliberately "—what didn't you do?"

Chapter 11

Lacey let herself into her office building shortly after eight Monday evening. She had promised Margaret she would help plan the second-time bridal shower for Lilah McCabe. Not that Margaret really needed any help, Lacey mused as she switched on a light and plodded wearily across the reception area. Margaret was such a whiz at organizing social gatherings she could probably do it with her eyes shut and one hand tied behind her back. Margaret was just trying to get Lacey's mind off the break-up with Jackson. If one could even call it that, Lacey amended dispiritedly to herself, since they'd never been officially together.

Sighing, Lacey slipped through the door and into the hall that led to her private office. And that was when she became dizzily aware of the all-too-familiar scent of Jackson McCabe's aftershave. Get a grip, Lacey told herself sternly as she bypassed first one examining room and then another. *Jackson isn't here. He left town three days ago, and he isn't coming back.* The fact she wanted him back was of no importance, Lacey thought as she turned the corner and stepped into her private office.

It should have been empty. Instead, there was a familiar figure—in jeans and a Ralph Lauren work shirt—in the chair behind her desk, sitting with his boot-clad feet propped up over the edge. He had his hands clasped behind him and a lazy, roguish grin on his face. Her heart slammed against her ribs.

"What are you doing here?" she demanded. Though she already knew she'd been set up. By Margaret and Jackson, no less! Would wonders never cease?

"Exactly what you think," Jackson said confidently. "I've come to see you."

And love her like there was no tomorrow and then break her heart again? Not a chance! Her mood growing even more irritable, Lacey gripped one rock-hard jeans-clad leg and knocked it off her desk. "We said all we had to say to each other last week."

And just to prove how immune she was to his charms, she sat down on the edge of her desk, facing him, and folded her arms in front of her.

"You may have," Jackson drawled, hooking a hand around her waist, and sliding her implacably down into his lap. "But I sure didn't."

Lacey gritted her teeth and retained her outward cool. It wasn't easy when he was looking at her as if he was planning to make her his again, on terms that were strictly his! "Let me go," she ordered quietly, pushing the words between her teeth.

Jackson shook his head. There was a decidedly rapacious gleam in his eyes, and an anticipatory curve to his sensual mouth. "Not until you hear me out."

Lacey felt her heart do a flip-flop in her chest. This bounder just turned your life upside-down and walked away, she reminded herself firmly. Don't let him do it again. "Fine." She shrugged as if she couldn't care less. Then followed it with a cool stare. "Start talking."

"I'm the kind of guy who likes to finish what he starts," he said, his expression unyielding and arrogant as hell.

His bold pronouncement made her feel caught off guard again, like she might not ever get her equilibrium back where he was concerned. Ignoring the faintly possessive way he was holding her around the waist, Lacey tilted her chin at him defiantly. "We did that." They'd felt an attraction, acted on it rashly and taken it to the bittersweet completion of breaking up. She saw no reason on this earth to do any of that again—even if he had made her feel as though she was and would always be the only woman on earth for him and vice versa.

Jackson paused, tightened his grip on her and eyed her thoughtfully. "No, Lacey, we didn't. But we can now if you'll give me half a chance." Keeping one hand on her, he reached behind him and brought out a gaily wrapped gift box.

Lacey stared at it as if it had grown two heads. "What's this?" If there was another sexy come-hither dress in there for her—that he wanted her to wear just for him—he was really dead meat. Bad enough to have two nights she would remember the rest of her life, without adding another one!

His lips curving into a bad-boy smile, he prodded, "Why don't you open it and see?"

Lacey moaned, beginning to get an idea where all this was going. "Jackson, I don't want presents from you." Especially ones inspired by guilt. "And I don't want you doing any more seducing."

"Then what do you want?" Jackson demanded softly, his eyes on hers.

Love. Marriage. All those things that will never work out for us, Lacey thought miserably. She closed her eyes briefly. "I want us not to hurt each other anymore."

"I'm all for that," he said gently, rubbing a hand up and down her spine.

Lacey could see the desire in his eyes. The shiver inside her intensified. Aware just how close she was to surrendering herself to him on any terms, she volleyed back breathlessly, "Then you can see why—with you just starting your new job in Fort Worth and me still here—we shouldn't do this."

Jackson studied the flush in her cheeks as he let his hand sift down the length of her honey-blond hair. "What I see is that geography shouldn't enter at all into whether or not we want to be together. And I do want to be with you, Lacey," he said in a voice not to be denied. "Now open this box and peek at what's inside."

Lacey drew a tremulous breath. Was it possible Jackson regretted their breakup as much as she did? Was it possible he wanted to go back, start all over again and do things differently, too? Her hand stayed

on the ribbon. There was only one way to find out, and
that involved sacrificing her pride.

Lacey licked her lips, knowing it was now or never,
and that pride was an easy thing to let go of, given all
that was at stake. Gathering her courage around her
like an invisible cloak, she splayed her hands across
the strong, solid wall of Jackson's chest and whispered,
"Suppose I had a change of heart. Suppose I was willing now to consider at least trying a long-distance sort
of I'll-see-you-when-I-see-you type of relationship with
you." Lacey swallowed. "Would you consider it?"

Jackson shook his head and his mouth twisted in
a rueful grin. "No, darlin', I wouldn't. I've had time
to think about it the past few days, and I've decided I
want you with me all the time, no matter what it takes
to make that happen."

*Like me, giving up everything here, just to be with
you,* Lacey thought. But was that so bad? Was it actually good? Lacey watched as Jackson's head dipped
and tilted toward her mouth. Knowing she would be
lost forever if she closed her eyes and yielded to his
kiss, she clamped her lips shut and turned her head
away

"We're different," she murmured as she dropped her
gaze to the curve of his shoulder.

Jackson smiled and she caught it out of the corner
of her eye.

"Different can be good," he said.

Lacey drew another, even more tremulous breath.
Someone had to exhibit some common sense, some
caution here! Swallowing hard, she reminded him, "We
bring out the worst—"

"—and the best—" Jackson added with a cocky smile.

"—in each other," Lacey finished with a sigh.

"And that can be good, too." Jackson rubbed her lower lip with his thumb. "'Cause we need to learn more about ourselves, and we need to grow if we're going to be any kind of parents to our kids. But I'm getting ahead of myself here." He stopped and nodded at the present in her lap. "Open the box, Lacey."

Lacey swallowed hard around the knot of emotion in her throat. *Might as well,* she thought. *He's not going to leave here till I do.* Her fingers trembled as she wrestled with the wide satin ribbon, then the lid. Inside were layers of tissue paper and a gift certificate from Lockhart's Boutique: "Good for one dress, any style, size or price and accessories."

Lacey worked to contain her disappointment. So he'd just been in the market for another sure-fire aphrodisiac after all. Damn it all, she'd wanted to mean more to him than that. She wanted to be more than his occasional friend and mistress!

He continued to study her, his look one of complete fascination. He began to grin his sexy, boyish, mischief-and-lust look she loved so much. "I figured you'd want to pick it out yourself," he explained.

Well, Jenna could use the business and the advertisement, Lacey thought. And she'd begun to agree with her mother—it was time she bought herself a few more new clothes. Not a lot. She didn't see why she should have racks full of things she barely ever wore. But a pretty new dress or two or three—that she could easily cotton to. "Thank you."

"Now open this," Jackson continued solemnly.

He handed her an envelope. Inside were two round-trip tickets to Cancún and posh hotel reservations, also for two. This was looking more and more like he expected her to be his mistress, and a jet-setting one at that! Lacey's heart began a slow, heavy beat. "Jackson—"

"I'm not done yet, darlin'." Silencing her with a finger to her lips, Jackson reached into his shirt pocket and brought out a rectangular-shaped velvet jewelry box that could have held a pair of earrings or a necklace, maybe even a broach or a tennis bracelet. Whatever it was it was too large for a simple engagement ring. Regarding it, Lacey's spirits plummeted all the more.

"Before you render any judgment, you have to take a look at this."

Lacey opened the box. She stared down at the contents in utter amazement and for a moment was too overcome with emotion to say anything, for inside were two matching wedding bands and a diamond engagement ring. She looked up at him, stunned speechless and dangerously close to bursting into tears of joy.

"If we're getting married, we've got to have the rings," he said gruffly.

Lacey swallowed as he slowly lowered his mouth to hers, relishing every inch of anticipation. "Who said we're getting married?" she teased as his lips closed over hers, once and then again and again.

"Me," Jackson said as he sighed and lifted his lips from hers. "And don't argue with me, 'cause it's gonna happen—" he predicted "—as soon as we get our license."

Lacey blushed with heat from head to toe, aware she had never been happier. "Oh, it is, is it?" she replied, loving the way he thought. There were some things they didn't need to wait on. This was one of them.

"Yep."

Lacey grinned. One heartbeat passed. Then another. They couldn't seem to stop staring at each other, or marveling at the sheer wonder of their togetherness. "And how do you figure that?" she asked in a soft, urgent voice filled with love.

"Because we've got Jenna Lockhart standing by, waiting to make your wedding dress, and the rings *and* the blessings from both our families—"

"Our families don't know about it," Lacey interrupted happily, aware everything in the world suddenly felt right again, now that Jackson was back in her life.

"They suspect," Jackson corrected, "and when they do hear it's definite, they'll be overjoyed."

Still... "Aren't you forgetting a few things?" Lacey asked dryly.

"Such as—?" Jackson lowered his mouth to hers and delivered a masterfully possessive kiss.

"Where we're going to live." Lacey regarded him expectantly, ready now to make the sacrifices she should have made before.

"That's easy." Jackson grinned his most wicked grin. "Laramie."

"B-but you said," Lacey sputtered as he ran his hands up and down her spine.

Jackson cut her off with a nod. "I know what I said

about having to have challenges." His eyes darkened seriously and his low voice filled with all the love and tenderness he felt for her. "I was a fool. The only challenge I need is right here in Laramie. It doesn't matter where I practice medicine, Lacey, so long as I'm helping people, and I can do that here as well as Fort Worth or anywhere else. What matters is being with the woman I love and letting the world know how I feel about her. What matters is having the opportunity to have children with the woman I love and to be able to see the family we already have on a regular— hell, even a daily!-basis. It took me almost losing you to make me see it, but everything I need—everything I've ever wanted, is right here in the little town where I grew up. So, for once and for all, to make it official—" he slid her off his lap and got down on bended knee in front of her "—Lacey, will you marry me?"

"Yes." Tears of happiness streaming down her face, Lacey drew him to his feet and wreathed her arms about his neck. "Oh, yes!"

McCabe family tradition demanded everyone be present for Lacey and Jackson's whirlwind wedding. So three days later they all gathered at the ranch. "You are one lucky guy," Jackson's brother Wade, who was serving as his best man, whispered in his ear as the bride made her grand entrance to the accompaniment of the wedding march.

"Don't I know it," Jackson murmured back as Lacey glided toward him. In a white-satin-and-lace, off-the-shoulder dress, designed for her by Jenna Lockhart, Lacey had never looked more beautiful or feminine.

She was going to make all his dreams come true, and he was going to do the same for her.

Lacey stopped beneath the flower-covered lattice-work archway. They turned to face each other, all the love they felt for each other in their eyes.

"I, Lacey, take thee Jackson...to have and to hold... from this day forward. I promise to love and cherish you in plenty and want, in joy and in sorrow, in sickness and health, for as long as we both shall live..."

"I, Jackson, take thee Lacey to be my lawful wife... I promise to love and cherish you in plenty and in want, in joy and in sorrow, in sickness and health, for as long as we both shall live..."

Rings were exchanged.

The minister smiled. "I now prounounce you man and wife. Jackson, you may kiss your bride."

In the hush that followed, Jackson swept Lacey into his arms. "My bride," he murmured, looking down at her, wanting there to be no doubt in her mind about the depth of his feelings for her. "I like the sound of that," he whispered as he held her tight, the soft surrender of her body against his a balm to his soul he'd be enjoying the rest of his life.

Lacey lifted her face to his. "So do I."

Jackson kissed her—the way he'd wanted to kiss her from the very first second he'd laid eyes on her—and the crowd around them erupted in laughter, applause and whoops of joy.

Beaming, Lilah McCabe turned to her husband and clasped his hand, her pleasure at having one of her four sons married apparent to one and all. "One down," she murmured happily.

John McCabe nodded in satisfaction as he cast a glance at their other boys. He squeezed Lilah's hand. "Three to go."

* * * * *